# ENTANGLED

**ELIZABETH
ROSE**

Copyright 2024 by Elizabeth Rose

Cover by RJ Caron Wolf Moon Press

Published by Oliver Heber Books

9781648397011

PUBLISHER'S NOTE: This is a work of fiction. Names, characters, places, and incidents either are the product of the author's imagination or are used fictitiously. Any resemblance to actual persons, living or dead, business establishments, events, or locales is entirely coincidental.

Copyright © 2024 by Elizabeth Rose Krejcik

Cover art by Dar Albert at Wicked Smart Designs

Published by Oliver-Heber Books

0 9 8 7 6 5 4 3 2 1

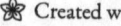 Created with Vellum

# One

Merrow Havfine stretched out lazily atop a rock, closing her eyes and basking in the hot summer sun. Such warmth never felt so good. The light illuminated her face as well as her barely-clad body. The melodic splashing sounds of the ocean waves lapped at the sea stack beneath her. This rocky outcrop was her favorite resting spot. It also served as a preferred gathering area for the rest of her forty-nine sisters.

Being an undine, or sea nymph, made her extremely comfortable in the water. She was one with the element. A guardian of the Aegean Sea. This was her home amongst dolphins, sea turtles, and exotic fish of every size and color. Merrow had grown up with her forty-nine sisters and one brother. They all took care of each other since her mother disappeared years ago, and her father, Nereus, was usually busy since he was known as king of the sea.

A tugging sensation on her foot caused Merrow to open one sleepy eye to find her favorite sister, Galene, playfully surfacing from beneath the sea. She spouted a stream of water from her mouth, hitting Merrow right in the face. It made them both laugh. Galene silently called Merrow back into the water without even having to use words. The undines had no real powers except for the ability to converse with each other through their minds, and shapeshift into humans while on land.

The undines were all beautiful women who wore thin, wispy clothing that clung to their wet bodies, not slowing them down at all in the water when they swam.

"Galene, you know I'd love to play but this is my special time for sunning myself. With so many sisters, we need to keep to our schedules." Merrow liked order and was in charge of keeping her sisters in line. As one of the older sisters, her job was looking after the others and keeping them safe.

She smiled at her red-haired sister, seeing the mischief in Galene's bright blue-green gaze. All fifty of the sisters had the same color eyes that matched the gorgeous hue of the crystal clear waters of their home. All the water nymphs had long, flowing locks. Hair in shades of every color, with most of the girls having at least three hues intertwined. Merrow's long mane was a rich brown that glowed with interwoven streaks of pink and green. Her colors mimicked the bright coral and lush sea moss found at the Mystic Reef. The girls sometimes tied up their hair in braids or ornate knots. Merrow liked to leave her hair long and free, letting it fall past her shoulders to flow out in the water around her as she swam beneath the surface.

"Please, Merrow, Melite and I want to follow Ephyra, Arethusa, and Panopea, to the Mystic Reef to search for pretty shells."

"Sister, you and Melite are women now, and no longer children," Merrow reminded her, reaching over to brush a wet lock of hair behind her sister's ear. Merrow played the role of mother to her younger sisters, knowing each of their strengths and weaknesses better than even her own. "You should be tending to your underwater chores instead of being distracted by pretty baubles."

Melite's head came up from under the water next. She had a round face and blonde hair and was even younger than Galene. Still, they were both women and no longer children.

"Please, take us there," begged Melite. "You know the fastest way around the jagged rocks and how to avoid the sharks so they won't chase us away."

"Yes, you do. Better than anyone," agreed Galene.

"Of course, I do," Merrow answered. "And when you've had as many years as I've had to practice, you'll be as skilled at underwater maneuvers as well. One hundred and fifty years was how long Merrow had been practicing. The life expectancy for humans would never even come close to matching this number, but undines lived at least one hundred years past this age. While Merrow was one hundred and fifty, to humans she looked comparable to a twenty-five year old woman.

"Then you'll take us?" Melite's sweet eyes were filled with hope.

"You know Father doesn't allow you to go near the Mystic Reef. Or, at least, not until you're older. It's much too dangerous out there. Besides, the weather is too unstable. Not to mention, sometimes strange things happen at the reef. Scary things," she added sadly.

"We know, you don't need to remind us," said Melite with a sigh. "Our mother went there one day and then something happened and she disappeared. But that was a long time ago."

It had been eight years now since the disappearance of their dear mother. "I overheard some of our sisters saying Mother left on purpose and nothing bad happened to her," Melite continued.

3

"Hush!" spat Merrow, pushing up to a sitting position. She scanned the area quickly. "Don't ever let Father hear you say that. It will make him angry. Believe me, you don't want to feel his wrath."

"Father isn't anywhere near. He's not listening," said Melite innocently.

"Mayhap not now, but you both know that Nerites is his eyes and ears. If he hears this nonsense, he'll report it back to Father in the blink of an eye."

"Why can't our brother be more like his sisters?" asked Galene with a pout. "Nerites is always snitching on us."

"He watches over us. That's different," Merrow assured her sisters.

"You watch over us, Merrow. All he does is cause trouble." Melite pouted now as well. "Take us to the reef. Please."

"It'll be all right. You'll be there to protect us," Galene urged her. "We know we're safe with you."

"Plus, Ephyra won't get so angry with us if you are there to soothe things over." Melite rested her arms on the rock, her body still submerged.

"Yes, Merrow," agreed Galene, attaching a bright pink sea anemone to her long braid. "You always have a way of maintaining peace between all of our sisters."

"Well, I'm not sure it's a good idea to go there." Merrow sat up straighter, noticing the scent of a storm in the air. The squall was quickly approaching. The clouds darkened above them, taking on an angry composure. It wouldn't be long now before the sky opened up and rain pelted down all around them.

"We can be there and back before the storm approaches," said Melite, knowing Merrow's thoughts though Merrow hadn't expressed them aloud.

"Nay. We can't possibly swim there and back before

the storm approaches." Merrow frowned, wishing for her sunshine to reappear. Nothing made her feel happier than sun warming her face while she dangled her toes into the cool waters.

"Not in that form you can't, Merrow. Of course, not. Don't be silly. You have your human legs and they'll just slow you down." Galene hoisted herself out of the water and onto the rocks, her long tail flipping back and forth in the growing breeze. The iridescent scales of green, purple and gold reflected the light. Undines had tails like mermaids while in the water, but once they were on land, they looked and walked on two legs like humans.

"Hurry, Merrow. Get into your undine form," urged Melite. "You know you can swim faster than any of us by using your tail."

"I'm not sure I agree to this idea." Merrow looked over her shoulder to the other side of the rock where another dozen of their sisters were sunbathing but starting to slip back into the water one by one because of the approaching weather. "Nerites watches us closely. Too closely. We can't risk him reporting back to Father that we're breaking the rules. It'll get us into a lot of trouble."

"Since when are you afraid of trouble? Besides, our brother is checking on the fishing boats right now, and keeping the rest of our sisters away from their nets," Galene pointed out. "Nerites won't even know we left for the reef. He has his hands full with all his responsibilities. It will take him some time to check on all his fifty sisters."

"She's right. Plus, he can't swim half as fast as we can. Come on, Merrow. Do it!" Melite continued to coax her. "I only need a few more of those pretty pink shells found only at the reef, to complete my necklace.

Plus, I want to try to attract my personal shell charm to me, now that I've come of age."

The undines, when old enough, attracted a personal shell charm from the sea to them. It was usually a soft shell that could sometimes even feel feathery. It would connect to their essence and become part of them in every way. It helped to hold their emotions and their feelings at bay. Most of all, it helped to control their sexual prowess since sea nymphs were very sensual, sexual creatures. The undines wore the personal shell charm in their hair. It was something that stayed with them always. It would help to give them strength and control. However, if for some reason it was ever taken from them, it could bring about a horrible fate.

Melite lifted the strand of shells around her neck, clicking them together. "If we wait any longer, the storm will cover all the shells with silt and we'll have to wait another week until the sea bottom settles in order to go after them again."

Merrow ran a hand through her hair that had been dried by the sun, glancing up at the sky once more. Even though she was the best at caring for others and maintaining order, deep down she got tired of always being the responsible one. Undines didn't have souls. However, if she had one, she was sure it would be reminding her that she really did enjoy taking risks and exploring new areas. It was a longing deep inside her that always called to her and kept her alive. The Mystic Reef seemed to constantly beckon her. At times she was awoken from a deep sleep, swearing she heard her mother calling to her from the reef, even though it wasn't so.

Merrow loved all her sisters as well as her brother, but Melite and Galene were her favorites by far. She would do anything to make them happy. Seeing them smile made Merrow's heart sing. Plus, it helped ease the sting of no longer having a mother, as well as putting up with an ever-absent father. Merrow was close to her sisters and would do anything to keep that bond strong.

"All right," she finally answered with a wink. "Why not? I haven't done anything exciting in a long time now. If we're fast, we'll find your pink shells and also be able to attract your personal shell charm as well. We can beat the storm, and be back before Nerites even knows we're gone." Slipping into the water, her mermaid-like tail instantly appeared. The tips of her ears grew longer and fin-like. Webbing appeared between her fingers and toes that would aid her in moving through the water in a sleek and rapid way. "Let's go." She dove into the sea, not even bothering to take a breath. Undines could breathe under the water or breathe air while on land. They had the ability to do both. However, in the water was where they gained their strength and energy and where they always felt their best.

The lingering rays of sunlight streamed down, lighting up the hidden underwater paradise that Merrow had grown up in and always loved. With Melite and Galene right behind her, Merrow purposely held back as she swam so she wouldn't lose them in her wake. Instead, she drank in the beauty of the underwater life all around her.

Schools of red mullet fish darted one way and then the other as she came through. Their bright hues of red, pink and orange always reminded her of the sun. A wrasse fish followed her as she swam. This was one of the most colorful fish in the sea in green and blue with red dots that made up stripes. Bottlenose dolphins smiled at her as they encircled her, wanting to play a game of chase. Merrow made a face at some of the puffer fish, blowing air into her cheeks trying to mimic the way they could blow up so easily.

She continued to swim, nodding to a garfish at the ocean floor. Its slim, long snake-like body curled around a rock while its needle nose poked at something beneath the sandy floor. Merrow reached out and dragged her hand across the back of a large sea turtle as it slowly floated past, biting at seaweed and underwater fauna along the way. She swam along with a dusky grouper, a black scorpion fish and even a blue spotted bream.

The waters of their home were so blue and clear. Little islands dotted the area, and Merrow knew each one of them like the back of her hand.

After passing some blue crabs in a nearby lagoon, they came to the Mystic Reef filled with the most colorful coral ever known. It made her happy to see it. She'd heard of humans who painted, and this was none other than the sea painting its beautiful colors below the water, splashing them onto the ancient coral reef. Merrow stopped and held up a hand, telling her sisters to wait. She didn't want to speak with her mind or the others would hear her.

She thought she saw a glimpse of someone swim by in the distance, but when she spun around to look, there was no one there.

*What is it, Merrow?* asked Melite using her mind to communicate anyway.

Merrow held a finger to her lips and nodded toward their sisters, Ephyra, Arethusa and Panopea who had finished gathering up the coral and shells into their baskets, having sensed the approaching storm. She waited until they swam off before leading Melite and Galene toward the Mystic Reef.

*Collect your shells quickly*, she told her sisters, feeling a cold chill wash through her and it wasn't from the frigid water. Something wasn't right. She felt it in her bones. There was danger approaching, but she couldn't place from where it came.

While Galene and Melite scooped up shells and placed them into the bags slung over their shoulders, Merrow kept a close watch. Once again, she thought, or sensed someone or something watching them. She spun around, but didn't even see a single fish anymore. It was much too calm around the Mystic Reef. Calmer than usual. She supposed the underwater sea creatures sensed the approaching storm and that is why they remained hidden.

*Hurry,* she told her sisters, noticing Melite clicking the pink shells together. A large smile spread across her face.

*These are the biggest and best shells we've ever found,* said Melite. *This will make the best necklace I've ever had in my life. Now, I just need to try to attract my personal shell charm to me.*

Thunder boomed overhead, sending the vibrations flitting through the water. Looking up to the surface, Merrow could see flashes of lightning in the sky. She was about to tell her sisters it was time to leave when she looked behind her and her mouth fell open in shock. The water at the reef started to swirl violently making what she could only explain as an underwater sideways funnel. Colors of green and blue lit up the inside of the swirls and glowed from within with a fuzzy white color. Then, to her horror, she saw her sisters being pulled toward it.

"What's happening?" asked Galene aloud, using her voice instead of her mind to communicate now. She struggled to swim away, but it was like a very strong current.

"Help!" cried Melite, shoving the rest of the shells into her pouch as her body was swept toward the swirling waters that started to open wider now. It was some kind of underwater portal!

"Hold on, I'm coming," Merrow yelled to her sisters. Even though she was a strong enough swimmer to bring herself out of this strong current, her sisters were not. She didn't think twice about risking her own life to save them.

"Merrow, help us!" Galene's eyes opened wide and her hand shot out as her tail was sucked into the water portal and she started to disappear.

"I'm scared!" cried Melite, trying to swim upward, but the portal sucked her right to it as well.

"I won't let that thing harm you!" With all her might, Merrow swam right toward the portal, reaching out and grasping each of her sisters by the arm just as they started to slip away. She pulled with all her might, but the water portal was just too powerful. She would have to either let go of her sisters to save herself, or surrender to the swirling water, just to stay with Melite and Galene.

She chose the latter, not willing to leave her siblings who were in dire need of her protection. Still holding on to them securely, she relaxed her body, letting the water pull all three of them deep into the center of the portal.

Something caught her eye again, and she noticed their brother, Nerites swimming toward them just as the portal started to close.

"Nerites!" she shouted, but it was too late. The portal snapped shut before their brother could reach them. They were sucked through brackish waters that became so dark she could no longer see a thing. Still, Merrow held firmly to her sisters, not willing to let them go.

The crystal clear waters of home disappeared. They were now surrounded by dark waters and also the feeling of doom. They needed to get to the surface to see where they were. Merrow needed to get her bearings. "Swim to the surface," she instructed her sisters. They did as told, but Merrow never made it there. She felt a jerking motion and realized that her tail was entangled in some kind of netting that kept closing in around her, swallowing her up.

She was trapped and being pulled upward! The net enclosed her, making her a prisoner as it slowly dragged her along with it toward the surface.

Now Merrow knew what happened to their mother so many years ago. And she also felt it in her gut that she and her sisters were never, ever going back home.

*Two*

## LAND OF MURA

"T his is a waste of time. We're never going to catch anything." Zann Blackseed looked over the edge of his brother, Rhys' ship, The Spectrum, and shook his head in disgust. He and his brothers, Darium and Rhys, had been fishing for several hours now and all they'd caught was an old boot, a rotten log, and a lot of insults from Elric, Zann's father-by-marriage. Even Stone Nightstalker, the newest member of their group, wasn't having any luck.

"If you boys would just face the fact you stink at this and let me help, we'd all be home and eating a good meal by now." Elric leaned back against the side of the large fishing ship with his feet up and his arms crossed. His eyes were closed.

"Nay. We don't need your magic to put food on our tables," grumbled Darium, pulling in a line and lifting it up to see that it was empty.

"Zann and I are kings. We can provide for our people and especially our own families, Rhys chimed in.

"That's right. Besides, Stone and I can go out hunting later," offered Zann, just itching to get back into his shapeshifting form of a wolf to hunt at night in

13

the Goeften Forest. With Zann's animal instincts and Stone's clear night vision, they were bound to make some good catches.

"Stonestealer is a bounty hunter. He doesn't hunt animals, he hunts men," scoffed Elric with his eyes still shut. The short little elf was a sage and also messenger of the gods. He was probably the most magical of the beings of Mura, but also the most irritating. If Zann hadn't been married to the man's daughter, he and his brothers most likely wouldn't tolerate Elric and his vulgar ways.

"I'm no longer a bounty hunter, just a tracker," Stone answered in his defense. "And now that I'm married to your second daughter, I'd appreciate it if you called me by my real name. It's Nightstalker, not Stonestealer...Father." Stone added the latter part just to get a rise out of the elf.

Elric's eyes shot open and his mouth turned down into a nasty frown. He jumped up on the wooden seat, still no taller than Stone who was sitting, being no taller than waist-high to a common man. "Call me Father once more and you'll find out just how powerful my magic is when you're scraping your hind end off the bottom of the Masked Sea," spat Elric. "And don't think I can't do it."

"Calm down, Elric." Darium wound up his fishing line and wiped his hands on his breeches. "We're all family and need to get along now."

"I never wanted to be friends with a Sin Eater like you, Darium." Elric was at it again. Always seeming as if he longed to stir up trouble.

"I'm no longer a Sin Eater," said Darium. "And we don't have to be friends, but nothing can stop us from being family. So just get used to it."

"I told you we shouldn't have come out here to fish," Elric continued to complain.

"Only some of us are really fishing." Stone raised an eyebrow looking at his lazy new father-by-marriage. Stone's dog, Fang, jumped up from his sleeping position on the deck and ran over and hopped up on the bench next to Elric. The dog put his paws up on the side wall of the ship and looked over the edge and whined.

"What's the matter, boy?" Stone ran a hand over his dog's head. "Something's got him spooked."

"It's probably all you big oafs pretending to be fishermen when none of you can even manage to catch a cold," said Elric, chuckling at his own jest.

"There's a storm approaching." Darium looked up to the mast of the ship, seeing his raven, Murk, landing atop the lookout basket and squawking like crazy. "Something's got Murk upset as well. Mayhap we should pull in the net and start heading back. Hopefully, we can beat the rain."

"Sounds like the first good idea today." Elric jumped down from the bench, but did nothing to help pull in the net.

"Nay, I don't want to leave yet." Rhys stretched his neck, looking toward the other fishing ship close by. "I'm not leaving until he does."

"He, who?" asked Elric with a yawn. His short arms went out to the sides as he stretched, having just woken up from a nap. Elric hadn't even been invited on this trip but insisted he come along, just wanting to be nosy.

"Rhys only wanted to fish today because he saw King Ravenwolf's ship sail out earlier. Everything's got to be a competition with my brother," grumbled Zann.

Zann and Rhys had replaced two of the dead, evil kings of Mura. King Sethor had been the last one left but he recently died as well. At his death, Macada Castle was taken over by Sethor's nephew, Sebastian Ravenwolf. Sebastian was a much younger man than Sethor and also more capable of putting together a bigger and stronger army than his uncle. Rhys worried about King Ravenwolf storming their castles of Kasculbough and Evandorm and his brothers knew it.

"Rhys, it's starting to rain." Darium struggled to reel in the net. Zann and Stone helped him. "It must have tangled on something." Fang started to bark uncontrollably. The raven still squawked from the lookout basket above their heads. "We need to hurry and head back."

"I don't want this new king to think we are weak rulers." Rhys' stubborn side showed. "A little longer won't kill us."

"Nay, but I might." The elf crossed his arms over his chest. "Especially if the mutt doesn't stop barking. He's hurting my ears." The little man placed his hands over his pointy ears and cringed.

"He's sensing something wrong. I know my dog," said Stone, still petting Fang and looking over toward the other king's ship. "I feel it too. Something is fishy."

"Not a good jest considering we didn't catch a thing today," said Darium, still pulling on the net, not understanding what it could be stuck on.

"Nay. That's not what I mean. King Ravenwolf has caught something. Whatever it is, it seems pretty big. Take a look." Stone pointed toward the other ship. King Ravenwolf's men were hoisting up the fishing net and it looked to be loaded.

* * *

"Pull harder! Raise that net now," commanded Sebastian Ravenwolf, running to the edge of the ship to see if they'd perhaps caught a dolphin or two in their nets. They'd had bad luck all day, and Sebastian hadn't wanted to retreat until Kings Zann and Rhys brought in their nets as well. He was the new king of Macada Castle now since his uncle's demise. He needed to prove his worth to the Blackseed brothers, since those boys had magic on their side and he did not. Mayhap his catch of a dolphin would make his enemies see him as more of an equal after all.

"My king, the nets are heavy and the men are tired," said his captain, Owaine. "Mayhap if we just rest a minute."

"Nay!" shouted Sebastian, running to look over the side of the ship. "In another minute we're going to be blown around by this storm and I don't want to lose our only catch of the day. Stand down. Let me do it." He pushed Owaine aside and took his place. "Jocet, Hitch, on the count of three," he called to his steward and squire who were also his good friends. "One...two...three!"

They all tugged together and managed to get the net up to the top of the side wall. Then with the help of his friends, they lifted it up and over. Sebastian's impetuous action sent the net and its contents slamming down atop the deck of the ship. At the same moment lightning streaked through the sky and a loud crash of thunder rent the air, shaking the entire ship. Rain pelted down like arrows from the sky. It fell so fast and hard that he needed to move closer to see what was actually tangled in his net.

Taking out his dagger, he ripped the net open. When he did, the biggest fish he'd ever seen slapped its large tail outward in defense, hitting him squarely in the jaw.

"Ow! That stings! The damned thing is going to die for that." He wanted to cry out from the pain, but wouldn't show weakness while with his men. He drew his sword to end the dolphin's life, raising the blade over his head, ready to bring it down with full force.

"Nay! Don't hurt me. Please," cried a woman's voice from the net. He stopped and looked down, his eyes opening in disbelief. There, in his net was a strange sea creature! From the waist up, his catch was a beautiful woman with long hair, full breasts beneath a thin bodice, a small waist and mesmerizing eyes. From the waist down, she was all fish.

"What is it, my king?" Hitch ran over, stopping in his tracks. "Is it something Belcoum spat up from the depths of the Dark Abyss?" he asked, referring to Mura's devil and hell.

"Nay, I can't say it is." Sebastian's eyes interlocked with the sea creature. He felt as if he couldn't look away even if he chose to do so. "I'd say it was someone sent from The Haven, by Zoroct," he replied, referring to Mura's Heaven and one of their main gods. "This woman looks to be no demon but more like a goddess of the sea."

* * *

Merrow's heart raced in fear. She lay helpless on the deck of the ship still in her sea nymph form so she wasn't even able to run away. Not that she'd have any-where to go to hide, since she was on a ship in the middle of the sea. But still, if she could manage to get close enough to the side wall, mayhap she could somehow flip over it and get back into the water. That was her only hope for escape. Water was her safe haven.

"What are you?" asked the man staring down at her. He was handsome for a human. Long, dark brown hair and light blue eyes. The hue of his eyes was close to the color of a sky on a cloudy day. She quickly glanced around. Nothing looked familiar. She wasn't sure where she'd ended up after being sucked through the portal. "Are you a demon or a deity perhaps?" asked the man.

"Nay! Of course, not." Merrow struggled to sit up. The storm continued and the rain washed down over her undine body. She'd never get her land legs at this rate. Not sitting out in the open and being doused by the rain. "I am an undine," she told them. Seeing the bewildered looks on all the men's faces, she got the feeling they'd never seen an undine before. They continued to stare at her with wide eyes and open mouths. She wasn't naked but she might have well been since her light clothing clung to her like a second skin, leaving nothing to the imagination. Slowly, she crossed her arms over her chest, trying to hide her breasts that were spilling out of her bodice.

"You're a what?" The man squinted one eye and cocked his head.

"An undine," she repeated, still seeing their empty gazes. "I'm a sea nymph." She struggled to try to pull herself across the wooden deck, using her arms alone. It wasn't easy. The deck was wet and her tail slippery. Getting over the side wall seemed an impossible task. She didn't make much headway at all.

"What did she say, Captain?" asked one of the crew.

"She called herself an imp, I think." The man who she supposed was the ship's captain scratched his head, looking over from the stern of the ship.

"I am not an imp, you fools!" These stupid men were trying her patience. All she wanted was to get off this ship and back into the water so she could find her sisters. "Can't you see that I am far from being a troublesome demon? And if I were a deity, I wouldn't still be here, trapped upon your boat."

"What is she saying?" one man asked the other, who just shrugged in response.

"King Ravenwolf, what exactly is she?" one man whispered to the handsome man who had almost killed her.

"Are you a...mermaid?" asked the man who they'd referred to as king. Well, at least one of them was getting closer with his guesses.

"Fine," she said, letting out a deep sigh. "I suppose I am similar to a mermaid, so just call me that if you'd like. It doesn't matter. All I care about are my sisters. Where are they? What did you do to them?" She flopped around on the deck, wishing the rain would stop so her legs would emerge. Merrow was at a disadvantage being in her aquatic form while on a ship filled with dangerous humans.

"Sisters? There are more of you?" asked the king, twisting around to look over the side of the ship and into the water again.

Merrow suddenly realized her mistake. She never should have said anything. Now, they'd be throwing their nets out again, hoping to catch Melite and Galene.

The wind roared and the sky became black now. It was a bad storm that threatened them and didn't look too promising to let up any time soon. The crew was having trouble handling the ship, keeping it from being blown and tossed about in the waves.

"Lower the sails to half-mast!" shouted the man who seemed to control the crew. He was an older man with a balding head. "If we don't head back to shore right now, my king, we're going to be plundered against the rocks and smashed to bits. We'll all die."

Secretly, Merrow hoped for that to happen. If so, she'd have a way to escape and look for her poor, frightened sisters, after all. She needed to protect them. That was more important than even her own well-being.

Also, she wanted them to know what happened to her. With her mind, she tried to speak to her sisters, hoping their fear of going through the underwater portal wasn't going to block their ability to talk to each other in this silent fashion.

At first, she heard nothing from them. Then, ever so faintly, she thought she heard Galene and Melite crying out for her in her mind. They called for her but she could do nothing to help them, and wasn't even sure she could reply. She concentrated, trying to hear their words in her mind. Then, she knew what they were saying, and it made her stomach clench. They, too, were caught in a net. Her head snapped back and forth, looking for a second net aboard this ship.

"How many fishing nets do you have in the water?" she demanded to know.

"Excuse me?" The king looked insulted or at least surprised that she should ask him such a thing.

"Is this your only net?" she asked. "Tell me. Quickly."

"It's the only one we've used today," answered the king. "Why does it even matter to you?"

She heard her sisters crying out to her again. From her position, she could barely make it out, since their voices were becoming softer. That meant they were moving away from her. She was sure now that there must be a second ship in the water. Her sisters were caught in a net, as well. There was no doubt in her mind.

"Whose ship is the other one?" she asked, seeming to surprise the king once again.

"How do you even know there's another ship?" he asked in suspicion.

The last thing she wanted was for him to realize she could communicate with her sisters by mind alone. "I'm a mermaid as you call me. I was in the water, was I not? I assure you, I know all that happens in the sea."

"Of course, that's how she knows." A man with scraggly brown hair standing next to the king nodded forcefully.

"Hitch, don't be a fool," the king answered. "She's lying."

"Sebastian, do you really think so?" whispered a blond-haired man standing on his other side. He was tall and lanky. He had facial hair that was short and trimmed. Merrow figured he was a close confident of the king to address him by his given name.

"Of course, she is," said the man they'd called Sebastian. "Because if she was truly so aware of everything that happens in the water, she never would have gotten caught in our net in the first place."

Merrow's eyes closed and she wet her lips with her tongue. This king was too sharp. It was almost as if he could see right through her, knowing if she spoke the truth or not. She longed to get away from him. She had to escape to find and help her sisters. Panic started to set in.

"My king, The Spectrum is hoisting up their net, so can we go back to shore now?" asked the captain.

"Did they catch anything?" asked Sebastian.

Merrow's eyes sprang open and she held her breath, waiting to hear the answer.

"Their net is on the other side of the ship and it is raining too hard to tell," shouted another of the crew.

"Then return to the castle," Sebastian gave the order, causing Merrow to release the breath she'd been holding. Even if she hadn't been able to help her sisters at the moment, at least the ship she was on decided to go back to shore. She was sure whoever caught her sisters was heading back as well. And once she got her land legs, no one would stop her from finding Melite and Galene. Nothing and no one was going to keep her away from her sisters, not even this arrogant king named Sebastian. Not if she could help it. As soon as they reached shore, she'd be gone before they knew what happened.

*Three*

Sebastian couldn't take his eyes off the mermaid as they sailed back to Macada Castle and docked the ship. The rain had let up slightly, but still it was coming down at a good pace.

"King Ravenwolf, my net is ruined." The captain looked down at the mermaid who was still sitting there, unable to move. The torn net was all around her. Trying to get untangled, she had ripped the thing to shreds.

"Owaine, stop complaining." Sebastian stomped over, his booted feet stopping so close to the girl's hand that she pulled it away and held it against her chest. "I'll buy you a new net."

"Well, what about that—thing?" Owaine pointed a finger at her. "What am I supposed to do with her? Filet the girl and bring her to your cook to prepare for supper?"

"What?" The undine, as the girl had referred to herself, gasped at the notion. She almost seemed to choke on her own spit. "I'm not a fish!" she finally managed to spit out. "You can't eat me."

"She sure looks like a fish to me with that long, plump tail." Two of the crewmen sidled up to her.

"I'm so hungry, I could eat her raw right now," said the other. "Forget the cooking."

"Before or after we have fun with her top half?" asked the first, and they both burst out laughing.

That angered Sebastian. His fist plowed into the first crewman's face, followed by his second punch, plundering the other disrespectful man as well. They both fell to the deck rubbing their jaws.

"If I ever hear anyone say something like that again, you'll be meeting with my blade instead of my fist next time. Do you all understand me?"

"Aye, my king." The men answered one by one, getting back to their duties.

"King Ravenwolf, you still didn't tell me what to do with her." Owaine waited for his answer.

"Nothing," he answered.

"Nothing?" Owaine shook his head and narrowed his eyes.

"I'll take her," said Sebastian, not wanting to leave the sea nymph with this crew. If he did, as soon as he turned his back they'd be spreading butter over her body and licking it off of her, no doubt. Damn, he cursed himself, now not able to get that thought from his head. As alluring as she was, he couldn't say he wasn't having the same fantasy of doing just that. Her perky breasts and taut nipples were showing right through her wet clothes, and he'd found it hard to look the other way. He reached down and scooped her up in his arms. Her hands clung to his shoulders and he felt her necklace made of shells and coral pushing up against him. Her long, beautiful and iridescent tail hung over one side while her long, unbound tri-colored hair spilled over his other arm.

He hurried across the pier, making his way past the small village huts and to the drawbridge of his castle. As he crossed, he spoke to her.

"Do you—do you have a name?" he asked, not knowing how to have conversation with a sea nymph since he'd never met one before.

"Of course, I do, you simpkin! I'm a person, too, you know."

"Are you?" He supposed that sounded dumb, even though he really wasn't sure if she was a person. Or just half a person. "Well, what's your name?" he quickly asked before she could call him a simpkin again for that last comment. He glanced down at the beautiful half-woman in his arms and waited for her to answer.

"It's Merrow. Merrow Havfine."

"Hello, Merrow. My name is—"

"King Sebastian Ravenwolf. I know," she answered, surprising him yet again.

"How did you know that? Oh. You heard my men. That's right." For some reason, he felt flustered around her and as if he couldn't even think straight.

"Of course," she answered snidely. "How else would I know?"

"Well, some of the beings of Mura are magical and can read minds. I wasn't sure if you could or not."

She jerked a little and her body stiffened. Something about that comment seemed to alarm her. "Mura?" she questioned as he crossed the drawbridge. People came running from all directions to see her. She shyly hid her face against his shoulder. It almost seemed as if she felt vulnerable right now. He supposed he couldn't blame her. "What is this land called Mura?" She peeked up at him with those translucent blue-green eyes that reminded him of the sea.

"Don't you know where you live?" he asked her. "Mura is the land that the Masked Sea surrounds."

"I have never heard of either of them before."

"You haven't?" He started wondering if the girl had

bumped her head and lost some memory. How could she never have heard of Mura or the Masked Sea? After all, that is where he'd caught her.

"Nay. I come from the Aegean Sea. Near Greece," she told him.

"I'm sorry, but you are making no sense right now. Back! Everyone back," he shouted, shooing away the onlookers. He wanted to speak to this creature in private. The only place to do so would be in his private solar. He hurried into the keep and up the stairs, kicking open the door to his chamber since his hands were full.

"Where are you taking me?" asked Merrow.

"Somewhere private." He turned and used his foot to close the door, not daring to loosen his grip, not wanting to drop the sea nymph. He walked over to his bed and gently laid her upon it. Sebastian stood up, wiping his wet hands on his tunic. His eyes fastened on her tail again. "I've heard of sea creatures such as you but have never before seen one."

"Stop staring at me as if I am naught but an oddity."

"But you are. Or at least you are in Mura. We don't have sea nymphs here." He turned and walked across the room to pour them each a glass of wine. "Tell me, what were you doing in the water?"

"Another stupid question. I'm a sea nymph. Of course, I live in the water. Is that so hard to understand?" came her muffled voice from the bed.

"I know that. But, how is it that you are from another land? How did you get here?" He filled both goblets and replaced the cork on the bottle of wine. He heard a soft padding across the floor. His instincts made him whirl around, his hand raising to catch her hand which held his dagger.

"Don't even think of it!" he spat through gritted teeth, realizing she had lifted his dagger as he carried her and was now trying to kill him with his own weapon. Such gall! He squeezed her wrist tight in his fist, causing her to drop the dagger. It clanged to the ground and she whimpered, trying to pull away from him.

Suddenly, he realized she was standing. How could she? His gaze lowered to find two long, beautiful shapely legs and bare feet. Her body was totally naked. The necklace of shells was all she wore. Her long hair covered each of her breasts, but he saw a thatch of tri-colored hair below her waist.

He quickly released her hand and took a step backwards. That is when he noticed the blood on the floor.

"You're bleeding."

"Yes. My desire to kill you backfired and ironically I am the one who was stabbed by the blade. When you made me drop the dagger, it sliced open my foot."

Sebastian groaned. "Damn. I didn't mean to hurt you."

"Didn't you." It was a statement, not a question.

"Please, clothe yourself and I will wrap your wound."

"With what?" she asked him, doing nothing to cover her nakedness. She seemed comfortable being this way and it made him wonder if all mermaids or sea nymphs ran around in the nude.

"You had clothes. Before."

"Yes. And I also had a tail, pointed ears, and webbed fingers and toes."

"I suppose you did," he said, realizing all her sea nymph features had disappeared and now she looked just like a human. "So...your clothes disappear when you—when you..."

"When I shift into my human form, yes," she finished for him, doing nothing to move.

"Doesn't being naked make you uncomfortable?"

he asked her, trying his hardest to look only at her face but it wasn't easy when she had such a shapely, inviting body.

"Should it make me uneasy for some reason?" was her wry remark.

"Nay, I guess not." Sebastian cleared his throat, feeling very uncomfortable in this position, even though he was the one who was clothed. He walked over to a trunk, opened the lid and pulled out a tunic and a pair of his breeches. He turned and handed them to her. "Here. You can wear these."

"Those clothes are made for a man." She looked down her nose at them as if they weren't good enough for her. It unnerved him. For some reason all that mattered was that he please her. He didn't know why he felt this way and wondered if it was a power of a sea nymph making him act like this. He'd have to ask her about it later. After she was fully clothed.

"Please. At least wear the tunic. You can wear it like a gown. I'll find you a cord to tie around your waist."

She reluctantly took it. "If you insist."

He put the breeches back and searched for a belt or rope of some kind, but she had a tiny waist and anything he could possibly give her would be much too large and bulky. "I'm sorry. I don't have a belt for you." He turned to see her standing next to his bed.

"Don't bother. I'll use this." She took the piece of yellow cord that held back the bedcurtains and tied it around her tiny waist. "Better?" she asked, holding out her arms and turning in a full circle.

Damn, the sea nymph had looked alluring in her mermaid form, but with legs he found her even more breathtaking. What in the world was the matter with him to be thinking about a sea creature in this way?

"Sit down and let me wrap up your foot." He ripped a piece of cloth, using it to bind her wound.

"It was a portal," she told him, reaching over and picking up his boar bristle brush from the table. Then she got up and walked over, sitting down on his bed. She ran the brush through her long hair.

"What?" His brain suddenly couldn't think. He didn't know what she meant.

"It was an underwater portal that opened up and sucked me and my s—I mean, sucked me through it, ending up here."

She had started to say something else and stopped herself. She was hiding something from him and he thought he knew what. "Yes, we have had portals mysteriously opening and closing here on Mura for a while now."

"Really?" The hairbrush stilled. "Has anyone like me every come through before now?"

"No. Not that I know of. Why?"

"No reason." She slowly brushed her locks once again.

"How did you sprout legs?" he blurted out, not knowing how any of this worked. "And what happened to your tail and your sea clothes? Where did they go?"

"When an undine is wet, we grow a tail and other means to transport ourselves through the water. As well as sea clothes. When we're dry that all disappears and we gain legs to walk on land. Like a human."

"But you're not. Human. Right?" He slowly walked over and picked up both goblets of wine, handing one to her.

"Nay, I'm not. You see, undines don't have a soul."

"They don't?"

She put down the brush and reached for the goblet. When she did so, a shell that was woven into her hair fell out and to the ground.

"Oh!" she cried, startled, forgetting about the wine. "I lost my personal shell charm." She started to reach for it, but he was faster than her.

"I'll get it," he offered, bending over and scooping it up in one hand. When he touched it, he felt a jolt go right through him. It was a cross between an orgasm and having all his senses explode at once. His eyes closed and he wavered back and forth. He wasn't certain that he wouldn't pass out.

"Give it to me. Give it back to me. Now!"

His eyes opened slowly. "Don't be upset. I wasn't stealing it from you." He looked down to see the shell glowing in his hand. He caressed it with his thumb, realizing it wasn't a shell at all. It held the form of one, but was soft. Spongey. It was also beautiful. It held an iridescent hue of green like sea water and brown like sand. It sparkled and felt warm to the touch. And every time he rubbed his thumb over it, it glowed brighter and brighter. "This is interesting. My touch seems to make it react by lighting up. Why is that?"

Sebastian looked down at the girl to see her eyes closed and her head thrown back. Her nipples were hard and poking up through his tunic that she wore. If he didn't know better, he'd say the girl looked to be sexually aroused.

"Merrow?" he asked, causing her eyes to snap open. "What's going on?"

"My shell charm." Her open palm reached out for it. "Drop it into my hand. Hurry. Right now."

"All right. Calm down." He was about to give it to her, but something made him stop and rub his fingers over it one more time. Sure enough, the shell lit up again. When it did, Merrow let out a moan of desire. She fell back on the bed with her hand between her legs, rocking back and forth.

"Merrow!" he gasped in surprise by what she was doing. At the sound of his voice, she shot up in bed, holding herself up with her arms, looking around.

"I'm sorry." She blinked several times in succession.

"You are acting this way because of this, aren't you?" He held the shell-like object out in front of her but she did nothing to retrieve it.

Her aqua eyes looked up at him, drawing him in, making him want to couple with her for his own pleasure. "Give it to me," she said in a breathy whisper. "Please. And I beg you not to stroke it again."

"Take it," he challenged her, still holding it out to her.

"I will." She reached out for it, but was pushed away by some invisible force. She fell back on the bed and let out a deep sigh. "You need to give it to me. I cannot take it from you." Her voice sounded sultry but weak.

"Why not?" he asked with a chuckle, sitting down with his goblet of wine still in his hand.

"I don't want to tell you." A little pout made her bottom lip stick out in the most alluring way. Without even thinking about it, he found himself reaching over and pressing his mouth up against hers. She tasted sweet and tangy at the same time. Her lips were full and ripe with sultry desire. Kissing a sea nymph was an experience like no other. It was so enlivening and exciting. What he felt in that simple kiss was something that he'd never forget as long as he lived. In her kiss he found not only erotic pleasure and passion, but he felt an energy come through her that almost made him feel connected to every living thing in the entire damned sea! Sebastian couldn't explain it, but for some reason it was...euphoric. He'd kissed a lot of women in his time, but never before had a simple kiss made him feel like this!

He quickly pulled back, afraid if he kissed her again,

he would lose control. Being a king, he couldn't let that happen. To do that would make him weak and vulnerable. He couldn't have that at all.

"Tell me what I want to know or you'll never get this back," he said in a half whisper. He taunted her by dangling the shell in front of her face since he knew now that she couldn't touch it unless he gave it to her.

"I don't want to tell you." She squeezed her eyes shut. He saw the struggle on her face. She wanted to tell him but didn't want him to know, all at the same time.

"Do it!" he commanded, causing her to jerk. Her eyes sprang open, interlocking with his. Neither of them seemed able to look away even if they had wanted to.

"All right. I'll tell you," she said softly, releasing a deep sigh. "That is my personal shell charm that holds all my desires, emotions and...wanton pleasures." When she said the latter, her voice dripped with lust if he wasn't mistaken. "It is meant to help a sea nymph keep in control. Especially since sea nymphs have a huge sexual appetite that can get out of control easily."

"Oh!" This time it was he whose body jerked. He almost dropped the damned shell when he heard her say that. Thinking about sea nymphs and sexual pleasures all at once was making him grow hard already.

She continued. "If a human takes an undine's personal shell charm, that human holds control over the undine, able to make her do whatever he wants."

"Whatever he wants," Sebastian repeated softly, his eyes drifting from her to the shell in his hand. Oh, this was all too tempting. "Forever?" he asked, curiously.

"Until the object is freely given back to them."

"Is that so?" He chuckled and took a drink of wine, liking the position he found himself in. After all, it wasn't every day a man could control the sexual desires of a sea nymph. "Hmm, this is interesting. Very interesting indeed." He cleared his throat, thinking how much fun he could have with this. "So, do sea nymphs have magical powers?"

"Nay. Not really. Besides a tail or legs emerging, that is." She said the words but since he was holding the shell that controlled her, he could tell she was lying. She had some kind of power but wasn't telling him about it. He wanted to know more, but his erection was getting uncomfortable. He decided not to press her about it right now. After all, he held all the power now that he had her personal shell charm. He could find out whatever he wanted to know later. Being a king, Sebastian craved as much power as he could possibly get, even if it was only power over a nymph of the sea.

"Have some wine," he said, handing her the goblet.

"Nay, I don't want any."

He rubbed his thumb over the charm. "Have some wine, I say."

Her head slowly lifted and those plump lips parted seductively. "Of course, my king. Whatever you want me to do," she said, taking the goblet from him. She drank down the wine in three gulps and handed the cup back to him. "Did that please you?" she asked him.

"Well, nay. I mean, not exactly." He played with the goblet, looking into the depth of the empty cup. He'd just controlled her, but for some reason it didn't make him feel as good as he thought it would. Something about it just didn't feel right. Sebastian couldn't understand it. Since when did power and control feel wrong? This is everything a king craved. It should have made him happy. He needed to get away from this girl and come back when he had a clear head.

"Where are you going?" she asked him as he headed for the door. "And why haven't you given me back my shell charm yet?"

"I need to decide what to do with you." He looked down to the shell charm in his hand, feeling confused and conflicted. Then he closed his fingers over it instead of giving it back to her. "I believe I'll hold on to this for now." His eyes sought her out and then his gaze returned to the undine's most precious possession, now in the palm of his hand.

"Nay. Please. Just put me back in the sea where I and my sisters belong." Her voice was frantic. She was begging.

He looked back at her once again. "Your sisters?" He raised a brow. "So, there are more of you then?"

She gasped and her hand covered her mouth but slowly dropped to her side. "I mean me. I meant just me." Her cheeks were red and he knew the effects of drinking the wine so fast must have made her careless with her words. She'd slipped up and told him one of her secrets.

"You asked about your sisters on the ship as well. Tell me about them."

"There's no getting anything past you, my mighty king, is there?" She sounded angry now. Merrow reached over and picked up her goblet from the table and downed that entire cup of wine as well, banging it back down when it was empty.

"You had sisters that came through the portal with you, didn't you?" Sebastian took two steps back into the center of the room. "There are more of you here. That is what you're worried about. You don't want me to find them. That is why you asked me if we had more than one net on the ship. Isn't it?"

"I don't know what you mean." She was acting cocky again and he didn't like that. He was a king and all his subjects needed to treat him with respect. He didn't tolerate lying.

He held up the shell in his hand and rubbed it hard, purposely showing her that she could no longer keep the truth from him. "I want to know everything, you little devious sea nymph. Tell me now. Did your sisters come through the portal with you or not?"

She looked at him with hooded eyes, slowly getting up off the bed and making her way toward him as if she were a predator stalking her prey. "Yes, my lord, that is correct. I had two sisters come through the portal with me and I will do anything to find and protect them," she told him in a monotone voice. It almost didn't even sound like her. Perhaps it was because she was telling him against her will. Mayhap he'd rubbed the charm too much or too hard.

Merrow gripped him by the front of his tunic and pulled him to her, slamming her lips up against his. She kissed him, bit at his lips, and her hands wandered over his body. She ripped open his tunic, her fingers gliding over his chest and biceps. Her fingers dug into his muscles, and then her nails scratched his skin. He meant to pull away, but she just kept on going. Her hands were at his belt, her fingers gliding over his clothes, causing his manhood to become even more erect. Dammit, he was so excited! He realized he had brought this on by rubbing her charm. He also realized that he really liked it. Damn, now she was controlling him. He couldn't have that. There was no way he was about to let her control his sexual urges even if that is all he could think about at the moment.

"Nay. Stop!" He pushed her away from him, releasing a deep breath.

"What's the matter?" she asked, batting her long, curvy lashes. "Isn't that what you wanted when you rubbed my shell charm so hard that it almost broke? And if you say no to me right now, I will know you are lying. We both see the proof." Her gaze slowly raked down every inch of his body, stopping at his protruding form sticking out from beneath his breeches.

"This is over. For now," he told her. "Now stay here. I am locking you in the room for your own protection."

"Give me my shell charm and I'll leave here on my own accord. I promise you will never have to see me again."

Sebastian never felt as confused as he did right now. He should have probably just given her the damned charm, but stubbornness made him cling to it even tighter now.

"I think not, my little mermaid. And don't try to control me again, because I'm a king and you will never succeed. I am much too wise and strong and powerful to fall for your little games. Ever."

He turned and left the room. When he was locking the door from the other side, he swore he heard her talking to herself inside the room. It was just a mumble, but it sounded to him as if she said, "We'll see how wise and strong you are when my father finds out what you've done."

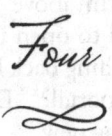

## Four

"Throw them back into the water, I tell you. They are only going to bring us trouble." Elric paced back and forth atop the wooden seat of The Spectrum, huffing and puffing in a fit of rage which was normal for the little man.

"Please, don't hurt us," cried the older-looking of the two sea nymphs that the Blackseed brothers and Stone had pulled out of the water, caught in their net.

"We need to find our sister," said the younger one with the blonde hair. She clung to the mermaid with the bright red hair.

Rhys had never seen anything like this. None of them had. "Who are you?" he asked in curiosity.

"I am Galene Havfine and this is my sister, Melite," said the redhead.

The men introduced themselves as well.

"We're looking for our sister, Merrow, who came through the portal with us," said Melite.

"Nay! Don't tell me there's more of you creatures?" snapped Elric. "Can this get any worse?"

"Portal?" all the rest of the men said at the same time, focusing on the true trouble here and it wasn't the girls.

39

"It was a frightening experience." Melite looked as if she were going to cry. "All I wanted to do was collect shells at the reef."

"There was a storm above the water and it must have caused the portal to open up where we were," explained Galene, smoothing back her sister's hair.

"An underwater portal?" Darium raised a brow. "Now, that is something new."

"No more portals," complained Zann with a swish of his hand through the air. "Can't we just live in peace for once?"

"You said there was another sister with you?" asked Rhys.

"Yes," answered Galene, sitting on the deck with Melite. Their tails flipped back and forth as a light rain continued to fall. "Merrow was pulled away from us. We need to find her and get home before our father finds out we disobeyed him and went to the Mystic Reef. If he discovers we went against his wishes, he's going to be very angry and it won't be a good thing."

"An angry father is the least of our worries right now," mumbled Stone.

"So, that must be what we saw Ravenwolf and his crew capture in their net." Rhys looked over to where The Thunderbolt, King Ravenwolf's ship was fishing, but it was no longer there. "I think they've got your sister."

"Merrow was captured?" gasped Melite.

"Never mind that," Stone broke in. "Tell us, where is your home?"

"We come from the Aegean Sea," Galene explained.

No response.

"By Greece," she added.

The men all shrugged.

"I'm sorry, but we've never heard of such a place." Darium was more than concerned.

"How do we know this portal isn't going to open up again and more of you won't come through?" asked Elric, zipping back and forth on the ship, moving so fast he made the rest of them dizzy.

"We're not really sure. We don't even know what made it open in the first place," explained Galene. "Please, can you help us find our sister? It's very important."

"Nay!" snapped Elric, the same time the rest of the men answered, "aye."

"We can take them back to Kasculbaugh." Rhys offered his castle.

"Nay. My castle is closer and it'll be faster. We'll dock at Evandorm," said Zann.

"What are we going to do with these fish girls?" Elric shook his head. "We're just inviting trouble by taking them back to the castle. They shouldn't even be here at all."

"We're undines," said Melite.

Silence again.

"Sea nymphs," added Galene.

"Oh, like a mermaid, right?" Zann looked them up and down. "I mean, we've heard of mermaids but have never actually seen one before."

"Something like that," answered Galene, shrieking when Fang came up behind her and started licking the back of her neck.

"Fang, get back here." Stone pulled his dog away.

"How are we going to transport them?" asked Zann. "We'll need to get a wagon."

"Nay, we will walk," answered Galene.

"Really." Darium looked over to his brothers and shrugged.

"Oh, no. Not like this, of course," said Galene with

a giggle. "We can only swim when we have our tails. But once we are dry and on land, our legs will emerge. We'll look and walk just like humans."

"I can't wait." Elric's words dripped with sarcasm. "Let's get back because I'm hungry for supper." He smiled evilly. "We're having fish."

* * *

Sebastian entered the great hall to meet up with his men later that day, having kept away from Merrow. He did not want to be near the lusty sea nymph. What he needed was to discuss the undine with his trusted men and figure out exactly what to do with her. Sebastian liked the idea of having a unique, not to mention beautiful, creature under his control. He also liked the fact he'd have something that the Blackseed brothers did not. After all, his late uncle always stressed to him that being king meant having and maintaining power. Uncle Leofric Sethor never wanted to be less powerful than any of the other kings of Mura. Especially not the Blackseed boys. Sebastian had to uphold that image and make his uncle proud of him. Even from the grave.

"My king, we hear you've captured a sea witch," said his advisor, Drell, approaching him with Sebastian's captain of the guard, Farrimond. Both these men were at least ten years older than Sebastian's twenty-five years. They'd been close allies of Sebastian's uncle. Sethor had always looked to these two for guidance while he served as king. Sebastian would do the same since they were the most experienced men at the castle. Sebastian had served in Sethor's army, but really knew nothing about being a ruler. Hopefully, these two men could help him uphold his inherited role of king.

"She's not a sea witch, she's an undine and her name

is Merrow." Sebastian took a tankard of ale from a serving wench and sat on his dais chair that was placed in front of the fire where he liked to sit and think.

"From whence did she come?" asked Farrimond, since neither of these two men were with him on the fishing ship when it happened.

"She came through an underwater portal." Hitch, Sebastian's good friend and also his squire, approached the fire, straddling a wooden bench while holding a bowl of grapes. "Would you care for grapes, my lord?" He held out the bowl but Sebastian shook his head. The last thing on his mind right now was food.

"My lord," said his steward, Jocet, approaching the table as well. His cook followed behind him with a large cleaver in his hand. The cook was a silent man, not able to talk since his tongue had been cut out by Sethor years ago for making a dish that Sethor said was rancid although Cook argued that it was fine. King Sethor had told Cook that his sense of taste was lacking and his tongue should be used for testing food instead of speaking back to a king. By right, he should have been executed, but Sethor was a nasty man and thought it would be more fun to cut out the cook's tongue and continue to make him work preparing food. He couldn't taste the food but neither could he argue or talk back to a king anymore either.

"What is it, Jocet?" Sebastian took another swig of ale.

"Cook wants to know how to prepare mermaid. He wants me to ask you if it should be roasted or basted for the best flavor, now that he has no way of actually tasting the dish first."

"Nay!" shouted Sebastian, almost choking on his ale. "No one is going to touch Merrow. If anyone should even try, they'll answer directly to me, and I promise the results will be grave. Understand?" He looked directly at Cook when he spoke, angry with him for even suggesting such a horrible thing. Jocet was Cook's voice since the man couldn't speak, but there was nothing wrong with his ears. "Understand?" he said once again, waiting for an answer.

"Aye, my lord," the men around him all answered one after another. Cook nodded forcefully and bowed before turning and running back to the kitchen.

"Oh!" He heard a feminine voice cry out, followed by the sound of two bodies hitting the floor and a loud clank. He looked over his shoulder and groaned. Merrow was prone on the ground and so was Cook. Cook had dropped his cleaver. Merrow's bare legs had every man's attention, since her knees were bent and her legs were not together. "I'm sorry. I'm not as skilled at walking as I am with swimming. I didn't mean to bump into you. Will you forgive me?"

Of course, Cook didn't answer, since he couldn't.

"Please, say something. I feel awful." Merrow jumped up, picking up the cleaver and holding it out to Cook. "I think you dropped this."

"Zoroct's eyes, nay," Sebastian ground out, using the name of one of Mura's gods in his curse. He handed his ale to his squire and bolted across the room, grabbing the blade from her. "I'll take that," he said. "Cook, get back to the kitchen." The man wanted his chopping blade back but Sebastian didn't think it was a good idea. "You'll get it later. Now go!"

He grabbed Merrow by the arm and all but dragged her to the long, wooden trestle table in front of the fire. "I told you to stay in my solar until I returned. Plus, I locked the door. How did you get out?"

"I have many skills, including picking locks," she told him. "Coral spikes work well." She proudly fingered the necklace she wore made of shells, coral, and other sea life type things. Besides, you left me there, all but forgotten, and I was hungry."

"I see," he said, actually impressed by her cleverness on land, even though her home was in the water. "Sit down here by me, and be quiet." He guided her to take a seat next to his squire. He handed the cleaver to one of his men passing by. "Take that to Cook," he said under his breath, not wanting the damned blade anywhere near this beautiful woman. If she suddenly sprouted a tail again, he couldn't trust that his men wouldn't want to kill and eat her after all.

"Want a grape?" asked Hitch, holding out the bowl to her as he raised the tankard to his mouth. Hitch was a few years younger than Sebastian, but much more care-free and reckless. Sebastian always calculated each and every one of his moves, constantly thinking three steps in advance, never wanting surprises. He liked to be prepared for whatever came his way. However, catching a sea nymph and bringing her back to Macada Castle was nothing he could have ever even dreamed of doing. He had no idea what to do with her, or how to take care of her for that matter.

"Oh, thank you, I'd love one. I am so hungry." Merrow daintily plucked a grape from the bowl and held it while she took a small nibble and sucked out the juice. "Mmmm, this is soooo delicious. I've never had one before. It tastes similar to a grub, but sweeter." She looked so happy. So innocent. And so damned sexy wearing his tunic and sucking on a grape, that he couldn't think straight right now if he tried.

"Squire, give me my ale!" Sebastian ripped the cup away from Hitch and drank down the liquid.

"So, this is the sea witch I've heard the crew talking about," said Drell, tapping his chin with one long finger. "I thought she'd look more like a fish and less like a human."

"She's most likely dangerous. We know nothing about her," commented Farrimond, watching Merrow with squinted eyes and a pursed mouth. "My king, you need to throw her back into the ocean anon."

"Yes!" Merrow popped the rest of the grape into her mouth and jumped up. "I'd like that, thank you."

"Nay," answered Sebastian in a deep voice. "The girl will stay at my side day and night until I can decide what to do with her."

Merrow slowly sat back down, looking defeated.

"I've been meaning to ask you. How was the fishing trip, my good king?" asked Drell. "Did you catch anything besides...this monstrosity?" He looked down his long but crooked nose at Merrow. It made Sebastian want to punch him for referring to Merrow in such a manner. But Drell was his advisor. Sebastian would be better off trying to befriend the man instead.

"Nothing worth talking about." Sebastian thunked down his tankard and stood up and stretched. It was late in the day but not nearly time to go to bed yet. He would have to come up with something to do that wouldn't be hampered by having Merrow along. "Jocet, borrow a gown for Merrow to wear from one of the ladies of the castle and bring it up to my solar. I won't have her walking around looking like a strumpet."

"Yes, my lord," said his steward with a bow of his head.

"Also assign her a handmaid."

"Yes, my lord."

"Oh, that's not necessary," protested Merrow. "I like to do things for myself."

"I can see that." Sebastian's eyes drifted back to her necklace she'd used to pick the locked door. "Farrimond, assign a guard to keep watch over the girl outside my solar door whenever I'm not there."

"Aye, my lord." Farrimond exchanged glances with Drell. "So, the sea witch is a prisoner then? Will she be executed?"

"Stop calling her a sea witch," snapped Sebastian, walking over and taking Merrow's arm. "And quit asking so many questions. A king never needs to explain his actions to anyone."

"My king, we need to discuss this situation." Drell was dogging his heels. "This is going to create quite a stir in the kingdom. Especially since she is a magical being. We can't have that here. Your uncle wouldn't have allowed it."

"I don't wish to discuss this at the moment. I'll let you know when I am ready, now see to the other matters."

"As you wish, your majesty." Drell fell back as Sebastian continued on to his solar.

"Am I really your prisoner?" asked Merrow. They climbed the stairs together. "And are you going to execute me like Farrimond said?"

"First of all, I haven't decided yet if you are a prisoner, a guest, or just a burden. Second, Farrimond never said I would execute you, he only asked." Sebastian stopped in front of his closed door to speak with her. "And third, I want you to start listening to me and stop giving me trouble. I am a king. You do know what a king is, don't you? Do they have kings where you come from?"

"Yes, we do. I know all about kings. You don't need to explain."

"I'm guessing I'm probably the first king you've ever met."

. . .

Merrow rolled her eyes, not able to believe the pretentious self-importance of this man. She also found it amusing that he spoke to her as if she were some kind of naïve child.

"You don't need to address me like a child. I am an adult if I must remind you."

"I see." He opened the door and let her enter, then followed her into the room and closed the door behind him. "How old are you? I'm twenty-five."

"I'm older than you think." She walked over and plopped down on the plush mattress of the bed. Not really spending a lot of time on land, her legs became tired easily from walking.

He chuckled. "Oh, you're such an old lady."

"One hundred and fifty."

"What?" His head snapped around and he made a face.

"My age is one hundred and fifty. Years," she added when he acted like he didn't understand. "Although to humans, I look to be about the same age as you."

"Nay. You can't be." He shook his head in disbelief and walked closer. "You don't look that old at all." He actually had the nerve to get close to her and bend over and peruse her face. He was probably looking for wrinkles.

"For an undine, that isn't old," she explained. "My kind can live up to two hundred and fifty years of age."

"You've got to be jesting!"

"Nay. Not at all." She picked up her necklace and played with it. "I, however, am one of the eldest siblings."

"By siblings, you're talking about those two sisters you're looking for. Right?"

"Yes. Them, and others."

"How many others?" He walked over and poured

himself a goblet of wine from a nearby table. "And do you have both brothers and sisters? I am an only child." He brought the goblet to his mouth.

"Yes," she answered. "I have one brother. And forty-nine sisters."

Sebastian spit a stream of wine across the room. Then he wiped his mouth with the back of his hand before he managed to speak. "Did you say...forty-nine? Or was it four? Or nine?"

"You heard me correctly the first time. I have forty-nine sisters, my lord."

"That's preposterous. You've got to be jesting."

"Well, mayhap you're right. I might have the count a little off," she said, thinking and looking into the air above her head. "Actually, my father has some daughters who are bastard children, so add about another dozen to that number of forty-nine, and that would be more accurate, I suppose."

He stood there with the goblet dangling from his fingers and his mouth hanging open. "I'd like to meet this mighty man someday. He must have an entire harem at his fingertips."

"Nay, you don't want to meet him. And what do you mean by harem?"

"I'm saying, he must have a lot of wives."

"Oh, that. Nay. Just one." She shook her head. "Except for a few mistresses through the years who produced the dozen bastard children. But otherwise, all of my true siblings come from the same woman."

"She, I wouldn't want to meet," he commented under his breath. "So all those sisters and only one brother? That's odd."

"Not really. It is more common for a sea nymph to birth girls. Nerites is the only boy in my family, besides my father, of course. My brother is very protective of all his sisters."

"I feel pity for the poor woman who had to bear all those children," he mumbled into his cup.

"My mother, Doris, disappeared years ago." Merrow jumped off the bed. "I think she might have been swallowed up by a portal like I was. Are you sure she isn't here?" She looked at him from the corner of her eye.

"Believe me. If there had been anyone like you here on Mura before, I wouldn't have forgotten about it. You are the first of your kind to walk this land...or swim this sea."

There came a knock at the door.

"Enter!" shouted Sebastian, doing nothing to open it himself.

"My lord?" His steward stuck his head into the room. "I've brought the handmaid and she has a gown for the nymph to wear."

"Good. Bring her in."

The handmaid walked in right behind the steward, and Merrow couldn't get a good look at her.

"The handmaid's name is Dee," said Jocet. "She'll be here to tend to the sea nymph's every need."

"That's not necessary. I'll just—oh!" Merrow almost fell over when the handmaid stepped forward holding the gown. This woman named Dee was anything but a servant of the King of Macada Castle. This woman was so much more. This handmaid was her missing mother.

*Five*

Merrow was about to cry out *Mother* but stopped as soon as she heard her mother's voice in her head.

*Don't let the others know who I am, Merrow. We can speak once they all leave.*

*Yes, Mother,* she said back, using her gift of telepathy to converse. *But I am so excited to see you, that I can barely keep from shouting aloud. Why are they calling you Dee?*

*I am not the same person anymore. Dee is what I go by now.*

"Why are you staring like that at the handmaid?" asked Sebastian, draining the goblet and putting it down on the table. "Jocet, Merrow said she doesn't want a handmaid, so send her away."

"Yes, my lord," answered his steward.

"Nay! Nay, my lord." Merrow held up a hand. "Leave her. I want a handmaid, after all. I need her. Please."

"That's not what you've been saying up until now." Sebastian took the gown from her mother. "Your services won't be needed, he told her.

"Please," Merrow begged Sebastian once again. "I

want, I mean I need, another woman to talk to. I beg you to leave the handmaid here."

Sebastian shrugged. "All right then. But there will be a guard posted at the door when I'm gone, so don't even think of trying to leave again. I'll be back in an hour. Come, Jocet," he said, and both the men left and closed the door behind them.

As soon as they did, Merrow barreled into her mother's arms, giving her a big hug. Tears ran down her cheeks. "Mother, I thought I'd never see you again. You've been gone for eight years now. We all thought you were dead."

"Merrow, darling, I am so happy we are finally reunited. I could hear your thoughts as soon as you entered the castle. So when the steward said he was looking for a handmaid, I was sure to volunteer."

"Were you swallowed up by an underwater portal, like I was?" asked Merrow.

"Yes. It happened one day when I visited the Mystic Reef."

"Father has never stopped looking for you. None of us have." Merrow walked over to the bed with her mother and they sat down together holding hands. "I asked Sebastian about you, but he said you weren't here."

"That's because King Sethor found me and kept me a secret from the others. I guess there were once three kings of Mura who didn't allow magic or dealing with magical-type beings at all."

"Have you been back to the sea?" Merrow asked her. "Mayhap we can sneak out of here together and try to find Melite and Galene."

"What? They are here too?" asked Dee.

"Yes. Melite wanted to hunt for pink shells and I

guided them to the Mystical Reef even though Father forbade them to go."

"You were wrong in doing so, Merrow." Hurt shone in her mother's eyes. "Now, because of your foolish ways, you and your sisters will be trapped here forever, just like me."

"Now that we're here, we can figure out a way to leave together," said Merrow. "You won't be trapped here any longer." Merrow always strived to stay positive and see the good in every situation and in all things. "We will find my sisters and then all go back to the sea. We will wait for the portal to open again, and then swim through and go home where we belong."

"Nay, Merrow. You don't understand. I can never leave. Never," said her mother.

"Never? I don't understand. Why not?"

"Because, I have lost my tail for good. I am human now."

Merrow's heart almost stilled. "Nay," she said in disbelief. "I thought the only time that happened to an undine was if we married a human. To gain a soul."

"That's right, dear."

"Mother, you are already married. To Father. So what are you saying?"

"I am saying that King Sethor stole my personal shell charm. When he did, he controlled me. He controlled my sexual prowess, and liked it so much that he made me get married to him. So, even though I have a soul now, I am trapped forever in the body of a human."

"Oh, Mother, that is awful. Father will be so angry that he will kill the man if he finds out."

"He won't need to. King Sethor was my husband, but now he is dead. He died going through another portal, so his evil deed was repaid, I guess."

"Oh, that's right. I heard it mentioned that Sethor

53

died going through a portal. And Sebastian is king now. He is Sethor's nephew, you know. But Sebastian is not an evil man like his uncle."

"I know Sebastian since I have lived here eight years, my dear. Sebastian will turn evil in time, just like his uncle, mark my words. All of the humans here are greedy and vengeful and they only care about themselves."

"Nay. I'm sure that's not true."

"It is, Merrow. I know you always try to see the good in everyone and everything, but remember you are no longer home. You are in a foreign, strange land now where people and things are different than what you're used to. Here, let me help you don this gown."

"If you were married to a king, why are you only a handmaid?" Merrow didn't understand.

"King Sethor was married to another woman as well as me, so he had to keep me a secret. His wife died a few years ago. Even after her death, he never told anyone we were married."

Merrow put her hands over her head and her mother pulled her gown into place. "There is no reason for you to stay here any longer, Mother. You will come home with me and my sisters. We will find a way."

"Nay, Merrow. I can never go home." Her mother lifted Merrow's hair gently, placing it outside of the gown. "I can never return, and you can never tell your father what really happened to me."

"So, you're saying that you want Father to go on believing you are dead?" This thought shocked Merrow.

Her mother nodded sadly. "It has to be that way. We cannot undo what has already been done."

"But what about my sisters? And Nerites? You want your own children to never know the truth either?"

"It is safer that way. You know your father's temper. We can't take the chance that one of your siblings will leak the information to him. It breaks my heart, but is the best for all of us. Everyone must go on believing that I am dead."

"Don't think that Father won't want you now, because he still will. I know he will."

"There you go with your positive outlook again. I admire it, Merrow, but you must come to the realization that just because you want something to happen, doesn't mean that it will."

"Give him a chance, Mother."

"I can't. I know that your father will start a war with the people of Mura over this. I won't allow innocents to die because of me."

"Mayhap you are wrong. Perhaps he won't do a thing. Since King Sethor is dead, Father won't need to start a war after all."

"He still will, and you know it."

"Oh, Mother this is awful. I finally found you and now I'm going to lose you again? I wish you could just come home."

"How can I? How can a union between a sea god and a human ever be?" asked her mother, causing Merrow's heart to feel as if it were breaking. "Besides, it would kill me to know that I could never be with my children under the water again. I would have to live ashore and watch from afar. I miss the sea, Merrow. I miss my old life. A life I can only covet but never have."

"Isn't there a way to reverse all this? Can't you somehow go back to being a sea nymph again?"

"Nay, there is not. When a sea nymph turns human, there is no reversing the decision."

"But this isn't fair. You were under an evil man's control," said Merrow. "This wasn't your choice at all."

"You are wrong, daughter. I did have a choice," said her mother. "I could have killed myself instead of living with that evil man as nothing but his human wife. Dying would have released me, but I just couldn't do it."

"Why? Did you have feelings for King Sethor?"

"Nay. Of course not. The only reason I did not kill myself was because hope still lived inside me."

"Hope? For what? Of coming home."

"Sadly, no. It was hope of being here if the portal should ever swallow up any of my children. I wanted to be here to help any of you from going through the same thing as me. And now, it has happened."

"So by that, are you saying you want to help us think of a way to get back home?"

"Yes. Even though I need to stay behind."

Her mother picked up a brush and ran it over Merrow's long, loose hair. "Merrow, where is your personal shell charm? It's not in your hair where sea nymphs are required to wear it. Did you lose it?"

"It fell out of my hair after I got here."

"Well, where is it?" Her mother looked around the floor. "We need to put it back in your hair at once. It is very important."

"We can't do that," she said, afraid to tell her mother the truth, but knowing she didn't have a choice. "Sebastian has it and will not give it back to me."

"Nay!" Her mother's knees buckled and Merrow had to catch her or she would have fallen to the ground. "Then, all my hope is dashed. My plan to help any of my daughters who ended up here has already failed. Because now, my sweet Merrow, you are doomed to repeat the horrors that I have lived through. You will never go back to the Aegean Sea, because that man will make you his wife and turn you human. And when he does, you will forever be under his control and will never be able to leave him."

* * *

"Merrow, are you ready to go?" Sebastian knocked quickly upon the door an hour later, but didn't wait for her to answer. A guard stood watch, so he knew she was in there. Plus, he could have sworn he heard talking and if he wasn't mistaken, even crying.

He pushed open the door to his solar to find Merrow with her arms wrapped around the damned handmaid. They both had tears running down their cheeks.

"What's going on here?" he asked, walking further into the room.

"Sebastian." Merrow sniffled, quickly wiped her tears with the back of her hand, and flashed him a fake smile. "I am dressed and ready to accompany you. Where are we headed? Off to find my sisters?"

"I had planned to go to the practice yard." He noticed the handmaid didn't look at him. That wasn't odd since servants were not supposed to meet with a superior's eyes. But he got the distinct feeling that the woman didn't like him. It made no sense since he didn't even know her. He recognized her as one of his uncle's servants, but Sebastian had never even spoken to the woman until today.

"Nay. We need to go and look for my sisters. It is vitally important." Merrow was a stubborn woman. He didn't like her telling him what to do, but supposed he could see why she'd be concerned.

"I'm sure your sisters are fine. They are probably in the sea. If so, we'll never find them, so searching is only a waste of time."

"That's not true." Merrow took his arm and led him to the door. The handmaid stayed at the bed fixing the blankets, her back to Sebastian, which he didn't like at all. It was disrespectful. He'd have to have a word with the handmaid later and reprimand her. "I can go in the water and look for them. I can call for them," she told him.

He could see what she was doing. She was planning her escape and he wouldn't fall for it.

"I'm afraid I can't let you do that."

"Why not?" The handmaid spoke up from the bedside. She looked directly at him, but quickly lowered her eyes when he looked her way. "Pardon me, my king. I beg your forgiveness for speaking out." She bowed deeply.

"Hmmm," said Sebastian, realizing something odd was going on here. Perhaps the sea nymph convinced the handmaid to help her escape. He'd have to keep a close eye on the two of them. "We will not be going back on the water any time soon."

"My lord," came a voice from the door. It was his advisor.

"What is it, Drell?"

"The Blackseed brothers and that irritating little elf are at the gates demanding to speak to you."

"Tell them I'm busy. Come, Merrow. We're going to the practice yard."

Drell cleared his throat.

"Was there something else?" Sebastian stopped in his tracks.

"It's just that they're asking if you caught a sea nymph while out fishing."

"Why are they asking me that?"

"I can't be certain, but Farrimond overheard them talking. It seems they have caught not one, but two sea nymphs as well."

"Oh!" gasped Dee from the bedside, hurriedly clasping her hand over her mouth and turning away.

"My sisters!" cried Merrow. "They found them. We

need to hurry down to the courtyard to talk to these people."

"Nay. Send them away," ordered Sebastian, not wanting anything to do with the Blackseed brothers. They were a thorn in his uncle's side for as long as Sebastian could remember. Plus, two of the three brothers took over the kingdoms of Kasculbough and Evandorm, and didn't deserve to be kings at all.

"But they have my sisters," cried Merrow. "Galene and Melite are worried about me. I need to see them and tell them I'm all right."

"Nay, I can't allow that. I'm sorry," said Sebastian. But before he could say more, Merrow pulled away from him and ran down the hall, disobeying him once again. His hand went to his pouch and he almost pulled out the shell, meaning to rub it and control her. Then he remembered how sexual she'd been when he did so last time, so he refrained from rubbing the shell with so many others around. "Let's go, Drell. If I'm going to talk to these Blackseed brothers, I'll need you to advise me on what to say. We'll grab Farrimond and a few dozen soldiers along the way. I am not prepared to fight off men who have magical powers."

Magical power wasn't what really had Sebastian worried right now. His biggest fear was that Merrow was going to want to go back home with her sisters. The last thing he wanted right now was for this beautiful, enticing sea nymph to leave him.

Then again, he reminded himself that he held all the power. So it was really up to him if she would stay or if she'd go.

## Six

"What do you Blackseed boys want?" asked Sebastian, approaching the small traveling party standing just inside his castle's gate. There were the three brothers and the elf. Sebastian had his advisor, captain of the guard, steward, squire, and several dozen soldiers backing him up. They all had their hands on their weapons, ready for a battle to break out.

"If you're looking for a fight, you'll get it," snarled Farrimond, starting to pull his sword. Sebastian raised his hand and stopped him from doing so.

"We come in peace." The Sin Eater, Darium, raised his hands in the air. Still, he had the power to control weather and didn't need a blade in his hand to be considered threatening.

"Peace? Hrumph," snorted Farrimond. "More than likely you're here to try to steal the last of the true kings of Mura's castles. Admit it."

"No one stole anyone's castle," spoke up Rhys. "I inherited Kasculbough from King Osric himself and you know it."

"And I married a queen and was elected King of Evandorm after King Grinwald's death," added Zann.

61

"I don't believe you," snapped Farrimond. Several of Sebastian's soldiers voiced their agreement with his captain of the guard.

"Men, stand down," commanded Sebastian, not wanting trouble. He directed his attention back to his visitors. "What is your purpose for being here?" he asked them once again.

"We need to know if you caught a sea nymph in your nets," said Zann.

"He did! It's me," Merrow blurted out before Sebastian could even respond. She ran forward to meet them.

"You're a sea nymph?" asked the elf from atop his horse. All of the Blackseeds were still mounted as well. "You look more like a lady of the castle to me."

"I look like one, but I assure you I am not. Did you find my sisters?" asked Merrow. "There were three of us who came through the portal."

"Quiet, Merrow, before I lock you back in your room again," threatened Sebastian, not wanting to look weak in front of the other kings. With the girl talking over him and asking questions before he could answer, it wasn't going to fare well with him where his enemies were concerned.

"We found two sea nymphs, but we don't want them," said the elf named Elric in his nasally little voice. The man was as small as a child, but Sebastian had seen him wield his powers before, and he was the most dangerous of the bunch of them. Sebastian needed to proceed cautiously and not get any of these magical people angry.

"Bring my sisters to me. Please," begged Merrow, once more talking over him. He couldn't let her get away with it again.

"That's it! I said to stay quiet but you can't seem to listen to directions," he told Merrow, losing his patience with her. "Jocet, take the girl back to my solar and be sure to post a guard and lock the door."

"Nay!" cried Merrow, fighting his steward. "I won't leave. I need to be brought to my sisters."

Sebastian had no choice. He needed to control her. Slipping his hand into his pouch, he quickly rubbed his fingers over the shell. "I said, you'll wait for me in my solar."

"Ooooo, I will," he heard her say in a lusty voice. "And when you get there, I will give you pleasure like you've never felt before."

"Huh?" Sebastian's head snapped around. Merrow was already untying her bodice. Damn, mayhap he rubbed the shell too hard again. He quickly released the charm, letting it drop back into his pouch. "Get her out of here," he ground out.

"Aye, my lord." His steward pulled her along with him. All the while Merrow looked back over her shoulder at Sebastian, throwing kisses. If he hadn't been embarrassed by her behavior before, he certainly was now.

"What was that all about?" asked Elric. "She's acting like your concubine."

"Never mind. Tell me, what do you want me to do about your sea nymphs?" asked Sebastian.

"Take them off our hands," said Elric, before the Blackseed boys had a chance to speak.

"Nay, that's not what we want at all," interrupted Rhys, the youngest, but biggest and strongest of the three men. He had super strength as his power and no one could best him in a fight. "All we want is to help the nymphs get back through the portal to go home."

"And how do you plan on doing that? Do the Blackseed brothers now have the ability to open and close portals too?" asked Drell.

"Nay. Of course not," said Zann. "No one can do that."

"Not true," said Elric. "I know someone who can."

"Elric, let us handle this," said Darium. "King Sebastian, we are willing to make a trade for your sea nymph."

"What do you have to offer?" Sebastian didn't plan on letting her go, but still, he wanted to hear what the Blackseed brothers were willing to give him. If it was a lot of money and gold, then he'd know that these sea nymphs were valuable creatures indeed.

"How about we give him Elric?" mumbled Zann under his breath.

"I heard that, you big oaf," snapped Elric. "You'd better watch it, or you'll be sorry."

"Elric, Zann is your son by marriage, he didn't mean anything by that," Rhys told the little man.

"You'd better hope not." Elric waved his hand in the air and a butcher's cleaver appeared.

Every one of Sebastian's men took that as an act of aggression and pulled their weapons as well.

"Elric, for Zoroct's sake, get rid of that, or we'll have a war on our hands," shouted Zann.

"What?" The elf looked around and shrugged. "I just meant don't get me mad or I won't cook your favorite meals for you anymore. Whatever." He nodded and the cleaver disappeared.

"I think we're done here," said Sebastian. "Guards, see our visitors to the gate."

"Wait! We're willing to pay you money for your nymph," said Zann as the guards escorted them to the exit.

"Not interested." Sebastian turned to leave.

"We'll get her one way or another, so don't think we won't," warned Elric. Then, in a blur, he sped away without his horse, so fast that no one knew where he even went.

"Where did he go?" asked Sebastian.

"I didn't see, did you?" Drell asked Farrimond.

"Nay, I didn't. Shall I have my men scour the area?" Farrimond asked Sebastian.

"Nay," Sebastian answered, looking over his shoulder as the Blackseeds left, taking the elf's horse with them. "Give me some time to think about all this. I am sure they won't try anything before daybreak. We'll revisit this matter in the morning. I'm going to bed, so make sure the gate is lowered and the drawbridge raised."

"Aye, my lord," answered Farrimond, talking to the soldiers and carrying out their orders.

Drell joined Sebastian. "My king, I must advise you that keeping the sea nymph will only bring you trouble."

"How so?" he asked as he continued walking back to the keep.

"You either need to give her up to the Blackseeds or we need to steal the other two nymphs and bring them here."

Sebastian stopped walking and turned back to his advisor. "Steal the other two? Why would I want three of them? One sea nymph is already proving to be more than enough trouble."

"Then give her up, my lord."

"Nay. I can't do that either."

"Then, our only choice is to own all three of them. If we do, we'll be true rulers. Mayhap these sea nymphs will have their own powers that we can use against the Blackseeds to conquer their castles and take over Mura for ourselves."

"We?" asked Sebastian, noticing his advisor was

using a lot of we's and ourselves. "Last I heard, I'm king, not you."

"Of course not, my lord, that's not what I meant." Drell chuckled nervously and bowed deeply, his hands pressed together. His cheeks turned red. "I just meant that it is what your uncle would do. I'm sure you want to follow in your uncle's footsteps in every way, don't you?"

"Yes. Of course, I do," said Sebastian, wondering if Drell was right. Three nymphs would give him the upper hand. Especially if the burdensome Blackseeds wanted them. He'd have to give this some thought overnight. "We will discuss this again on the morrow. Good night."

* * *

"Those other kings have Melite and Galene," Merrow told her mother, pacing back and forth in Sebastian's solar as her mother lit the candles and the fire on the hearth.

"Good. At least we know where they are now," her mother answered, poking the logs with a long iron rod.

"Mother, how can you say that is good? Who knows what they are doing to them. They could be locked in the dungeon and being tortured for all we know."

"Nay. They are safe with the Blackseeds, I assure you. They are good men. They are nothing like King Sethor or his nephew. Sebastian is the one you have to worry about, not them."

"And why is that?" came a deep voice from the door.

Merrow spun around to find Sebastian standing in the open doorway. "Sebastian! How long have you been standing there?"

"Long enough to know that my maidservant is speaking badly about me behind my back."

"I'm sorry, my lord." The iron rod fell from the woman's hand. "I didn't mean...I meant...I mean—"

"I think Merrow would be better off with a different maid servant. You are dismissed. Guard," he called out. "Take this maidservant out of here."

"Yes, my lord." The guard took Dee by the arm.

"Nay! I need her. Please, don't take away my maidservant," begged Merrow.

"You don't need her. And guard, you don't need to stand watch at my door tonight. I'll be here with the nymph so you are dismissed for now."

"Yes, my lord. Where shall I take this one?" He nodded at Dee.

"Take her to the dungeon for speaking ill of her king."

"The dungeon? Nay!" cried Merrow, feeling fear and dread wash through her. "You can't take her there. She is my m—"

*Nay, don't tell him, daughter,* came her mother's silent warning in her mind. *It will only be more dangerous for you if he knows.*

*But I can't let him hurt you, Mother. I won't let him put you in the dungeon,* she told her mother with her mind.

*It will be fine for now. Focus on finding your sisters.*

The guard left with her mother and closed the door. Merrow crossed her arms over her chest and glared at Sebastian.

"You've been a very bad girl today, Merrow." Sebastian sidled over to the door and slid the bar hold across and then used a key to actually lock it as well. He proceeded to drop the key into his pouch. "I don't like anyone speaking over me the way you did today. You are lucky I'm not locking you up in my dungeon along with that traitorous handmaid."

"She's not traitorous. You know nothing at all about her."

"I know enough." He unbuckled his weapon belt and took it off. "She and you were conspiring against me and that does not make me happy."

"All I want to do is to find my sisters. Yet, you will do nothing to help me. You are rotten, just like your uncle. Just like my m—maidservant said."

"I am not evil, and it hurts me to know that you think of me in that way." He hung his weapon belt on a hook on the wall.

There was a knock at the door. Sebastian went over and undid the bar and then unlocked the door and opened it slightly. "Thank you, Hitch. That will be all." He took a tray of food from his squire. There was also a bottle of something on the tray and Merrow figured it was wine. He held the tray in one hand while he bolted and locked the door once more.

"I'm a prisoner, even if you say I'm not. Just look at the way you bar and lock the door. That proves you are evil."

"Hush. I thought you might be hungry so I had food sent up. I know I am ravenous." He carried the tray of food over to a small table in the center of the room. Then he kicked off his boots and sat down on one of the two wooden chairs. "Join me," he said, holding out his hand, motioning to the food. He removed a dome from a plate and a delicious scent wafted through the air.

Merrow's stomach growled. She hadn't eaten since before they went through the portal, and was really hungry. "What is it?" she asked curiously, stretching her neck to see it.

"I thought you'd be more familiar with seafood, so I

ordered a pottage made up of scallops, lobster, oysters and clams. I also had some fresh white bread and some sweetmeats sent up as well."

"Seafood?" she asked curiously, moving closer ever so slowly.

"Yes. Or are they your friends and you can't eat them?" he asked with a half-cocked smile.

She let out a sigh. "Of course I eat seafood. That is my home. The fish and crustaceans of the sea gladly give up their lives to give my family sustenance. We just don't eat dolphins, octopuses, whales, sharks or sea turtles."

"And neither have I served you any. Now sit. Please."

"Well, mayhap just a bite." Merrow realized that Sebastian didn't seem rotten and evil right now. He actually seemed like he cared enough to offer her food, and that surprised her.

"Where are the shells?" she asked, looking around the tray.

"Shells?" She saw his hand go to his pouch that held her personal shell charm. The one that would enable him to control her sexual desires. He was careful not to let that out of his sight.

"Not that shell," she scoffed. "I mean the shells to scoop up the pottage so we can eat it."

He laughed heartily at that, and she didn't understand why.

"What is so funny?"

"You are," he told her. "Here on land, we use something called a spoon." He held up a metal stick with a round indention on the end. She stared. "You really never used the spoon before, have you?"

"I don't come to land often. And when I do, I don't eat, so no, I have never used a...a spoon or anything like it."

"Then allow me to show you how it works." He

used the indented end of the spoon to scoop up some pottage. Then he brought it to his lips, blew on it to cool it, and slipped the spoon with the food into his mouth. "Understand?"

"Of course I understand. I'm not addled!" She grabbed the spoon from him and tried to mimic his actions, but she forgot to blow on the food first. It was too hot to eat and she burned her mouth. "Ow!" she dropped the spoon and it went clattering to the table, spilling pottage everywhere. "I know how to use it, but I am not used to eating hot food," she told him. "My sisters and I eat the fish raw. We don't cook it."

"I see. Well, allow me to help you then." He repeated the process. Sebastian scooped up pottage onto the spoon, blew on the food, then slowly held it up to her mouth this time. "Open up, my little sea nymph."

Merrow opened her mouth and he slid the food into it. An explosion of delicious flavors accompanied by a spicy aroma awoke her senses and brought her to life. She closed her eyes and moaned at the taste of the rich and savory seafood pottage. "Mmmm," she moaned in pleasure. "That is soooo good." When she opened her eyes again, Sebastian was fidgeting on the chair. "What's the matter?" she asked him.

"Nothing." He fed her again, and she let him do it. Merrow enjoyed the intimacy of a handsome man spoon feeding her.

"Mmmm, ooooh, aaaah," she cooed, just loving the taste of this human way of eating food from the sea.

"That's it!" He threw down the spoon. "I can't do this anymore."

"What do you mean?"

As soon as he stood, she knew exactly what he meant. His aroused form was tenting out his breeches. She giggled.

"You think it's funny?" he asked, turning toward the fire. More than likely he felt too embarrassed to face her right now.

"What's funny is that you have my shell charm and supposedly can control my sexual urges and desires. Yet, all I did was eat food from a spoon and suddenly I am the one controlling yours. Humans sure are odd creatures." She ripped off a hunk of bread and gnawed on it.

"What exactly can I control by being owner of your charm?" He spoke to her over his shoulder, still not turning around.

"Owner?" She scowled at him.

"I mean, the holder of the shell."

"What exactly are you asking?" She was thirsty and uncorked the bottle.

"What I want to know is, can I actually control everything you do? And am I able to keep you here? Or is it just sexual matters than I am able to handle?"

"Keep me here?" she asked. "You want me stay?" She brought the bottle to her mouth, taking a swig, thinking it was wine. It wasn't. Fire burned her throat and she found herself unable to breathe. Choking and coughing, she ran to him for help, yanking on his arm until he turned around.

"Merrow? Are you all right?"

She was able to breathe air or breathe underwater. But right now, whatever that liquid was in the bottle, it stopped her from breathing in any way or form. She felt her head growing dizzy and gripped on to his arm so she wouldn't fall. Then, the next thing she knew, her eyes rolled back in her head and she felt her body going limp as she passed out against him.

# *Seven*

Sebastian carried Merrow over to the bed and laid her atop it. "Merrow? Can you hear me? Are you all right?" he asked. She didn't seem to be breathing and he wasn't sure what to do. It made him wonder about sea nymphs. Did they need air shared by a human? After all, if he were underwater, he'd need air from a mermaid to survive.

He could think of no other way to give her air than to blow it into her mouth. He lowered his head and did so, but the air came right out her nose and did not go into her lungs.

"Damn," he mumbled, holding her nose closed and trying it again. Success. This time, she coughed, and started breathing on her own. Her eyes shot open and he looked into those beautiful sea-colored orbs, hovering over her, so close that he could feel her breath on his face.

"Sebastian? What happened?" she asked in a sleepy voice.

"You drank some potent whisky and stopped breathing. No more of that for you. I had to share my breath with you to bring you back."

Her hand went to her lips. Then up to his face as she caressed his cheek. "You...kissed me. Didn't you?" she asked in a soft but shaky voice.

"I suppose you could say that. However, it was only to share my breath, I swear."

"That was so thoughtful of you. Thank you. I only wish I had been awake to experience the kiss like the last time."

"I wouldn't mind experiencing the kiss again either." He slowly brought his mouth to hers and gently kissed her once again. She tasted sweet, like honey, mixed with the tang of the whisky still on her tongue. He liked it. When she took his head in her hands and accepted the kiss instead of pushing him away, he found himself becoming excited. His eyes closed and his lips parted. He slipped his tongue into her mouth...and she bit him!

"Ow!" He pushed away. "What did you do that for?" He tasted the flavor of iron on his tongue.

"You were trying to choke me."

"Nay, I wasn't. It's a way of kissing. Don't mermaids know about it? After all, I figured being a sea nymph, you were probably a very sexual creature."

"How dare you say that!" She pushed up in the bed, hugging a pillow to her chest. "You make it sound as if I'm naught but a lush."

"I've heard tales about mermaids. They're usually naked from the waist up, aren't they? And sirens lure men to their deaths, first having their way with them. Am I wrong?"

"Don't even try to compare me to them. I'm not a mermaid or a siren. How many times do I need to tell you? And for your information, I am not a sex-starved woman."

"I said sexual, but it's the same thing." He brought her shell charm out of his pouch, holding it in his palm.

"What are you doing?" Her eyes grew wide, focusing on what he held. So much power to control her was right in the palm of his hand.

"I'm proving a point." He rubbed his thumb over the shell, and might have well been rubbing it over her womanly nub by the way she fell back on the bed and started squirming around in passion. He actually liked having so much control over her. Mayhap his Uncle Sethor was right. Having power was everything and anything that really mattered in life. "You like this, don't you?"

"Ooooh, yes!" She suddenly sat up and pulled off her gown, sitting before him totally naked. "I need to make love to you, Sebastian. Right now." Up on her knees, she reached out for him, pulling him hard against her chest and kissing him forcefully. He was surprised when her tongue shot out into in his mouth, the same way he had done to her just moments before. She proved to be a fast learner.

"You little vixen," he said with a low chuckle as she quickly reached out and pulled off his tunic, tossing it onto the bed. Then she pushed him to his back and into a prone position. "You, my dear, are proving to be even more sexual and sensual than what I've heard about mermaids."

"Is that so?" Merrow pulled off his trews and threw them to the floor. "Well, what have we got here?"

With his fingers still rubbing over the charm, Sebastian gasped when she ripped off his braies next. He felt the cool air against his hot skin. Then he felt so much more when she wrapped her fingers around his erect manhood.

"Mmmmm. So big and hard." The girl was out of control. She straddled him. "Do you know how constricting it is to have a tail?"

"Nay. I can't say I do."

"It feels so freeing to have legs to be able to spread!" She squealed and threw her arms in the air. "It is what every undine longs for. To feel the engorged manhood of a male entering into her body, sliding in and out, in and out." She undulated her hips with each word. Positioned directly above his erect manhood, she slowly started to slide down, ready to take him into her tight warmth. Sebastian wanted nothing more in the world than to make love with this enticing woman right now. He had never been so excited in his entire life.

He reached up with one hand, cupping her breast and squeezing. She giggled and cooed. Then his thumb grazed over her tight nipple. She moaned and threw back her head. Her long hair brushed against his arm. Merrow's skin was soft and smooth. Her breast felt full and firm. Slowly, he let his hand glide down her chest and belly, his fingers stopping below her waist. He eagerly played with her womanly folds, running the tips of his fingers through her downy curls. She was already wet and more than ready for him to slide into her so they could both experience their release. It would be ever so simple to do so. Every man longed for such a willing woman in bed. This one was throwing herself at him in want. This lovely sea wench wanted him just as much as he wanted her.

Or did she? Suddenly, this no longer felt right.

He felt a burning sensation against his palm, and glanced over to the shell in his other hand. It glowed a bright white. Guilt ate away at him. Merrow didn't truly want him in this manner at all. He was only fooling himself if he believed that to be true. The only reason the sea nymph was acting this way was because he was controlling her and making her do it! He'd initially only rubbed the shell charm to prove a point, but now this was getting out of control.

"Nay! Stop," he said, throwing the charm down upon the bed.

She was still atop him, straddling him. From this position he drank in the most glorious view of her firm, round breasts, taut little nipples and slim waist. His gaze traveled down her long torso to that thatch of curly hair at the juncture of her thighs that kept calling to him like a siren to a helpless sailor. Those long, glorious legs were wrapped around him and the contact of their bare skin felt hotter than ever. He grew even harder. Damn it, his lust for the nymph was so strong right now that it was driving him mad. Any other man would take what was being offered by such a beautiful woman in his bed and not question the feelings or emotions behind it. No man in his right mind would turn away from such a wonderful opportunity at a time like this.

Then again, Sebastian didn't want it if it wasn't real.

"That's enough," he growled, picking her up and setting her down next to him on the bed. "I've proven my point."

"W—what point?" She batted her eyes and looked around, seeming confused. Then she looked down and realized she was naked and scowled.

"You were controlling me, using my shell charm to make me want you, weren't you?" asked Merrow, disgust dripping from her words. She grabbed Sebastian's discarded tunic from the bed and quickly pulled it over her head to hide her nakedness from him. This man was an ogre to use her in this manner. How could he do such a thing? Especially after she explained to him the power he would have over her if he rubbed her shell charm.

"I'm sorry," he blurted out. "I never meant for things to go this far, it just sort of...happened."

"I don't believe you! And I certainly don't believe you are sorry at all for your actions."

"I stopped, Merrow. That should prove to you my words are sincere. I don't want to make love to you if down deep you don't really want to do it."

"Don't even pretend to know what I want or don't want. You are a worthless human being and a greedy, evil king who thinks of no one other than yourself!" She shot off the bed and paced the room.

"Is that really what you think of me?" He slid to the side of the bed and pulled on his trews, not bothering with the braies.

"Yes. Yes, it is."

"I stopped us from coupling," he pointed out once again. "Doesn't that mean anything at all to you?" He stood to tie his breeches.

"No, it doesn't because you also started all this in the first place if I must remind you."

"I said I was sorry. What else do you want from me?"

"How about letting me go? And setting Dee free from the dungeon as well."

"What?" He narrowed his eyes and shook his head. "Why in the world would I do that?"

"To show me you are not the cur I think you to be right now."

"If I did what you ask, what would my men think of me? Those actions would only make me look weak in their eyes. I am their king and ruler. I need to maintain a powerful composure." He scowled at her, walking over to a trunk and opening it. He chose a new tunic since she was wearing his. He could have asked for his back, but she was glad he hadn't. Sebastian pulled the tunic over his head, hiding from her view his strong and sturdy chest that she hadn't minded seeing in the least.

"What do you care what others think of you?" she asked him, holding her arms around her in a false sense of protection.

He straightened his tunic and blew air from his mouth. "I'm a king. Of course, I care. I have to care. I have expectations and an image to uphold. My late uncle's image. I can't let him down."

"Oh, I see. So, you idolize this dead evil uncle of yours so much that you are trying to be him now. That is pathetic."

His head jerked around and he faced her. "Nay. That's not true. Not at all." He slowly tied the strings at the neck of his tunic. "I am different from my uncle. I agree he was evil. He often liked to start wars for no reason at all. He also thrived on putting people away in the dungeon for no good reason in the least, keeping them there until they died from starvation."

"And you think you are nothing like him? Really." She sniffed. "You had no good reason to imprison Dee, yet you did. Sebastian Ravenwolf, you are quickly turning into this dead, evil King Sethor, no matter if you realize it or not."

"I most certainly am not!"

"Prove it," she challenged him. "Do what is right for the sake of goodness and being fair. Don't do things only because others expect it of you. Because you are afraid of letting them down."

"I'm not afraid of anyone or anything!" he shouted, shoving his feet into his boots. "How dare you say that about your king."

"You're not my king and will never be," she answered in a steady voice. Her words were upsetting him, and she didn't care. Someone needed to tell this man what a fool he was being, and that someone was her.

"Hush!" he spat, fastening his weapon belt around him. "I don't want to hear another word from you. And when I return in the morning, you'd better be here if you know what is good for you." He stormed over to the door.

"What's good for *me*? Or do you mean for *you*? After all, a king who does things only for the approval of others or because it is what he thinks he is expected to do, seems like a weak man indeed in my eyes."

"Don't say that," he warned her. His face became red with anger.

"Why not? Afraid of hearing the truth?"

"I told you, I'm not afraid of anything. Especially not you!" He opened the door and started to step out, but stopped. He turned and headed back into the room. For a minute, she thought he was coming back to her. To either kiss her again or mayhap slap her, she wasn't sure which. But he walked right past her without even slowing, only stopping when he got to the bed.

"You're never getting this back." Sebastian scooped up the shell charm from the bed and dropped it back into the pouch at his side. Then he continued to make his way back to the door. He stopped and spoke to her without turning his head to see her. "I'm locking the door and posting a guard so don't get any smart ideas." Then he finally turned his head ever so slowly, his eyes scaring her by their intensity. His loving or lustful gaze was gone. Now his eyes were filled with anger and revenge.

"Why are you looking at me that way?" she asked in a mere whisper.

"You, sea nymph, are never leaving Macada Castle, so just forget about ever going home."

Sebastian hurried down to the great hall, motioning for his advisor and his captain of the guard to join him at the dais.

"What is it, my king?" asked Farrimond.

"I thought you'd already retired for the evening," said Drell. "Is there something I can do for you?"

Farrimond had a tankard of ale in his hand. Sebastian ripped it away from him and took a long drink, throwing the metal cup to the side. "What kind of king do you two see me as?"

Drell and Farrimond exchanged glances. "My lord? I'm afraid we don't understand the question," said Drell, seeming reluctant to answer.

"You know exactly what I mean. Am I a strong king like my uncle was when he ruled?"

"I'm afraid you can't compare the two of you." Farrimond looked to the ground and shifted his weight, saying no more.

"You two think I am weak. Don't you?" Neither of them answered and that only made Sebastian even more furious. "Answer me!" he yelled, getting the attention of every man in the great hall.

"You know I only hold the highest regards for you, my lord," said Drell. "However, you don't seem to listen to my advice the way your uncle did. That, I'm sorry to say, does seem a little reckless."

"Reckless?" He looked at his head soldier next. "What about you, Farrimond? How do you see me?"

"Permission to speak freely, my lord?"

"Of course, you fool! I asked a question, now give me your answer."

"As a soldier, you were fearless. Very strong with a

blade in your hand. You fought to the bitter end and took orders well from your king. I'd say you were the perfect soldier."

"And now? Now that I'm king?" asked Sebastian, pressing the man to answer his question.

"Well, you don't seem to want to fight anymore." Farrimond's eyes flashed up and then back to the ground.

"What does that mean?" asked Sebastian. "Of course, I do. I just haven't had an opportunity to do so yet, that's all."

"I think having that damned elf and the bothersome Blackseed brothers right here in your courtyard was the perfect opportunity for a battle, yet you didn't take it. My lord," Drell quickly added the last part, probably trying to sound respectful, even though to Sebastian it seemed as if the man were chastising him instead.

"Battle? On what grounds?" he asked. "They didn't do anything to threaten me. They only asked about the sea nymph, that's all."

"The elf did manifest a cleaver," Farrimond mumbled.

"They want the sea nymph, and won't stop until they get her," Drell explained. "If I were you, my king, I'd storm their castle right away. Take their two sea nymphs instead. Do it, before you discover they've stolen yours from right under your nose."

"And you know they will," added Farrimond, nodding.

"Do you really believe they will do that?" Sebastian asked his men. They both nodded. Perhaps Sebastian should listen to them after all. They had many years of experience between them, yet he was new at being king and truly had a lot to learn.

"They won't have a chance to steal my sea nymph

because I won't let them," he told them, shaking his head.

"You...won't?" asked Farrimond, exchanging glances with Sebastian's advisor.

"Why not?" asked Drell.

"Men, we're going to put together an army to storm their castle at daybreak. I will take those two sea nymphs from them, and then I'll have three!"

"Yes! You'll hold all the power," agreed Drell with a satisfied smile. "That, my lord, is a brilliant idea. Now, you are thinking like a king."

"I agree. It is exactly what King Sethor would have done," said Farrimond. "I'll start organizing an attack party anon." Farrimond bowed and headed away.

"Yes." Sebastian nodded, trying to feel good about this decision, even though something in his gut told him not to agree with these two. "Be sure to post a guard at my solar door so the sea nymph doesn't escape," he called out to Farrimond.

"I am pleased you listened to my advice," said Drell with a low chuckle. "I knew you'd find your footing sooner or later."

"Then you think I'm really doing the right thing by going after the other sea nymphs?" asked Sebastian, having a wavering moment.

"Oh, I do," Drell answered. "You have taken the proper action expected of a strong king. I am happy to say that I wholeheartedly approve of your decision."

"Approve," Sebastian mumbled, walking away. It only brought to mind Merrow's accusation of him doing things only to be accepted by others. She didn't know what she was talking about. The sea nymph had no idea how hard it was to be king. He'd challenge anyone to try to do this job.

He pulled the charm out of his pouch, looking

down at it, letting out a deep sigh. He was doing the right thing, he told himself. A king had responsibilities. The ruler of Macada Castle didn't need a sea nymph getting in his head and confusing his mind. It was only a game she played with him. One to control him. Sebastian would never let anyone manipulate him, especially not a woman.

He raised his hand in the air, ready to throw down the damned shell charm and crush it beneath his heel. But just as he got ready to do so, he stopped. He pulled his hand back and looked at the vulnerable little shell in his hand, about to be crushed and having no way to stop his violent action. This charm was a part of Merrow she'd told him. By destroying it, he had no idea if he'd be hurting or possibly even killing a part of Merrow as well.

Thoughts of the kiss he shared with Merrow flitted through his brain. She was vulnerable and it was all his fault. When he controlled her, she had no way to stop things from happening. Was it right? He wondered. Sebastian, who had wanted her badly, now realized he only wanted her if she wanted him too. If he kept controlling her with this shell, he'd never know the true answer.

He lifted his hand again, meaning to throw down the shell and smash it once more. Then again, he stopped.

What if by smashing this charm that was so connected to her emotions and actions, he somehow kept her from ever feeling anything again? If that happened, he'd never forgive himself. She was so filled with life, and that was one thing he really liked about her. The poor girl didn't have anything much besides her feelings and emotions. Now he knew he couldn't smash the charm because Merrow didn't deserve to be hurt...or possibly to die.

He slowly slid the charm back into his pouch,

heading for his chair near the fire to spend the night. He could never go back to his own bed to sleep now. Not when he knew Merrow was in it.

It was his decision, but he couldn't be intimate with her again without first knowing the truth...if she could ever want him in the same way that he wanted her.

*Eight*

**M**errow snuck through the corridor, thankfully having been able to leave the solar before the guard even arrived at the door. She wore the gown of a lady now, covered by a cloak she'd found hanging from a hook on the wall.

It was Sebastian's cloak. She could feel his essence from the robe wrapped protectively around her. The scent of leather and woodsmoke clung to it, tantalizing her mind with each breath she took. Her head told her to be wary of this man. Not to trust him in the least. But her heart was singing a different tune. Mayhap it was only because she always tried to find the good in everyone and each situation, but she didn't believe Sebastian was truly evil. If he had been, he wouldn't have protected her from his men. She would be in the dungeon along with Dee right now, but he hadn't done that.

The cloak was two sizes too big for her and almost tripped her as she walked, but she didn't care. She needed a disguise in order to get down to the dungeon unnoticed. For some reason, being wrapped in Sebastian's cloak made her feel safe and protected, like being held in his warm and caring arms. It was similar to the same feeling she'd had when he carried her in her undine form into the keep after she'd gotten tangled in his fishing net. Or when he caught her when she collapsed in his arms. Nay, those weren't traits of a truly evil man. Were they?

She could tell there was a stir going on by all the commotion coming from the great hall. Keeping to the shadows, her curiosity got the best of her. She needed to know what was happening.

Hearing men's voices coming closer, she darted beneath the stairwell to wait until it was clear to emerge again without being seen.

"Our king requests I put together an army to storm Evandorm Castle at first light." It was Sebastian's captain of the guard speaking. There was no doubt about it.

"Aye, Captain. We will do whatever King Ravenwolf wants. But might I ask the reason for this battle?" asked a soldier.

"He wants the sea witches that the Blackseed brothers are harboring," answered Farrimond.

"There are more of them?" asked the soldier in surprise.

"Three in all." It was Drell who joined them. "Our king is finally acting strong like his uncle. With all three of the sea nymphs, he'll hold more power than any one of those Blackseeds."

"But the Blackseeds brothers have magic," said the soldier, sounding extremely concerned. "How can we fight that? We'll be at a disadvantage, won't we?"

"We will, but Sebastian won't let that stop him," said Drell. "He is too strong to be intimidated."

"The soldier has a point, Drell," said Farrimond. "We've all seen what kind of damage those magical beings can cause. And now all of the Blackseeds are married to women even more powerful than themselves. We will lose a lot of men going up against them."

"Then so be it," said Drell with no care at all in his voice. "The only thing that matters is that our king knows what is required of him and acts in the appropriate manner. Which he is doing, thankfully."

The men left and Merrow continued toward the dungeon, shaken to have overheard that conversation. It sounded as if Sebastian was still doing what he thought was expected of him. To gain the approval of others. Why couldn't he see that none of that mattered at all?

Luck was on her side. Just as she approached the outer room of the dungeon, the door opened and a guard walked past her, never even knowing she was there. Merrow held her breath, hiding in the dark corridor. As soon as he turned the corner, she rushed forward and slipped inside the outer room, only to see another guard. However, he was sitting on a chair balanced by two legs, leaning himself back against a wall. His feet were up on a table and his eyes were closed. She was sure he was asleep since she heard him snoring.

Carefully and quickly, she tiptoed to him, slipping the key ring from his belt.

*Mother? Mother I'm here to free you. Where are you?* she asked silently in her mind.

*Merrow? I'm in the first cell. But you shouldn't be here. It is too dangerous,* her mother answered back in her thoughts.

*Be ready to go. And stay quiet.* Merrow quickly found the key and opened the outer gate to the inner cells. The gate squeaked and her heart jumped. She held her breath, glancing back over her shoulder. Thankfully, the guard only stirred a little but was still asleep. Merrow saw her mother standing by the cell door. She opened it and together they walked hand-in-hand, sneaking out of the dungeon and into the corridor.

As soon as they were out of earshot, she spoke aloud. "Mother, are you all right?" She hugged her.

"I am fine, Merrow. You shouldn't have come."

"I couldn't leave you here to rot or to be executed."

"I appreciate the rescue, but where will we go now?"

"I overheard some of the men talking. Sebastian is putting together an army. He plans to storm Evandorm in the morning and steal Melite and Galene."

"You called the king Sebastian," said her mother, seeming bewildered. "Merrow, why would you do that? Have you been intimate with the man?"

"It's not what you think. Now hurry. We need to get there before them, and I have no idea where to even find Evandorm Castle."

"You don't, but I do. And I know exactly how we'll get there too."

Fifteen minutes later, Merrow and her mother were in a horse-drawn wagon heading toward Evandorm Castle. Her mother was driving.

"Tell me again, Mother. What is this wagon used for? It has a bad stench." Merrow looked over her shoulder to see shovels and rakes in a dirty wagon that looked as if it had never been cleaned.

"Every two weeks, a gong farmer comes to the castle at night to clean out the castle's garderobes," her mother explained. "We were lucky to have snuck out the hidden entrance and found the wagon while the farmer stopped to relieve himself."

"Gong farmer? Garderobe?" She looked back again and realization hit her. This was the man who cleaned up the human feces. "Eeeew."

"Humans have different ways of doing things since they live on land and not in the sea," answered her mother with a giggle.

They took a road in the dark that led to the Masked Sea. As soon as Merrow smelled the scent of water, she couldn't help her longing to be in it. "I want to stop and swim," she told her mother, not able to control the urge. "I long to be in the water again and feel as if I'll die if I don't do so right now."

"I understand." Her mother stopped the wagon at the beach. "You have been out of the water for a while and it'll help you regain your strength if you at least go for a fast swim."

"Thank you." Merrow smiled, already feeling better.

"Daughter, I don't know if I ever told you this, but undines need to swim at least every few days. If not, we become weak and will die."

"How can that be?" asked Merrow. "Do you go swimming that often?"

Her mother chuckled. "Nay, Merrow. I haven't been in the water since the day the portal brought me to Mura." She looked out over the water and in the reflection in her eyes from the moonlight Merrow saw a deep sadness within.

Her mother's story was horrifying to Merrow. Without her life in the water, or experiencing the feel and taste of it, she knew she would perish, just like her mother said. "Then why aren't you dead by now?" she brashly asked, needing to understand this completely.

"I am still alive because I married a human and gave up my life as an undine. I no longer need to be in the water at all." The sadness did not disappear.

"Oh, Mother! That is awful. Don't you miss the sea?"

"I admit that at times I still wish I had my tail and that I could swim underwater for hours at a time. But what I miss the most is your father and all my children." Dee put her arm around Merrow as they walked to the sea together. "There is a shorter way to get to the castle, but I wanted to come down this road to be by the sea once again. Plus, I did it for you, daughter. You need to go in the water now."

"I will," said Merrow, hurriedly undressing until she stood there naked. "Come with me," she begged, holding out her hand. "I will protect you, and you can at least experience the sea once again."

"Nay," said Dee, shaking her head. "As much as I want to, I am afraid I cannot. Over the years of being landbound, I have grown to fear the water and everything I once loved."

"Afraid?" Merrow chuckled this time. "Mother, this is the sea. Our home. It is where you bore fifty children, and raised them. It is a place that you always loved. How can you fear it?"

"This is not our sea, Merrow," her mother reminded her. "We are on Mura now. This is the Masked Sea. It is quite different. It doesn't feel the same. Now go. We don't have time to waste. We must find your sisters before King Ravenwolf does, if what you say is true. It seems the man only wants my children in order to be able to control them and to feel powerful in his own way." Sadness washed over her face once more. "I see now that King Ravenwolf is no different than his uncle in the least."

As much as Merrow wanted to talk more with her mother, her desire to swim and feel her tail again was calling to her. She couldn't ignore it. Stepping up to the water, she let the waves wash over her toes. It felt cool. Invigorating. Inviting.

Unable to hold back any longer, she dove into the water, feeling her shift swiftly happening beneath the waves. When she surfaced, she once again had a tail. It felt so damned good!

"I will be right back," she called out to her mother who was still standing on the beach. Merrow dove beneath the surface, swimming lower and lower, studying the fish and underwater fauna that was so different than that of her home.

She smiled and reached out to pet a dolphin passing by. Her long hair floated in the water around her. Wanting to explore more, she swam farther and lower, forgetting all about time. Then she came across a spot that seemed to be moving and shimmering. It swirled in a circle almost creating what looked like a tunnel. It was then that she realized it reminded her a lot of the portal that had brought them here.

Her eyes grew wide as a portal opened wider and wider until she could see someone peeking out from the other side. It was her brother.

"Nerites!" she called out to him. He floated through the portal and approached her.

"Merrow, I have been searching everywhere for you. Father is furious that you took your younger sisters to the Mystic Reef and now the three of you have disappeared. Thankfully, I saw what happened and told him about it." He looked around. "Where is Melite and Galene?"

"Nerites, how did you open the portal?" she asked instead of answering his question.

"Father was able to open the portal. He lent me his Calling Conch to use since he said that was what we needed in this situation. I remembered the vibrations of the water of the place you disappeared, and those vibrations led me here."

"It is so good to see you, brother." She wrapped her arms around him in a tight hug.

"Lead me to your sisters," said Nerites. "The portal will not remain open for long, and I can only use the conch shell to call upon it once every few days."

"Galene and Melite are not here in the water,"

Merrow told him. "They are landbound and at a castle. Mother and I are headed there to rescue them."

"Mother?" Nerites jerked backward in shock at hearing this.

"Yes, she is alive. But she is no longer an undine. She was forced to marry a human."

"Father will be furious to hear this." Her brother scowled, reminding her a lot of her father in one of his bad moods.

"Nay! You can't tell Father about this," she warned him.

"Why not? Mother is his wife. Of course, he has to know."

"Mother is also ashamed of what happened to her. She doesn't want Father to find out. She feels it is better if he, as well as our siblings, think she is really dead."

"And is that what you think, too?" Nerites shook his head, making no secret of how he felt.

Merrow wasn't sure how to answer. Then she thought of the love her parents once held for each other. It didn't feel fair. It wasn't right to keep them apart. Even after all that happened.

"I don't know if I agree with Mother, but it is her choice, not mine."

All of a sudden, Merrow heard her mother's voice calling to her in her mind. Nerites heard it as well.

"Nerites, something is wrong. Mother is trying to reach me. Come with me and help us. Please."

Nerites looked back to see the portal closing. "I can't," he said. "I need to get the Calling Conch back to Father or I might be trapped here as well."

"Then go," she told her brother. "But come back when you can. I will try to have our sisters ready to swim through the portal as soon as you open it again."

*Merrow, King Ravenwolf's soldiers have me. Stay hidden or they will find you, too.*

"Nay, Mother. I'm coming to help you. Hold on." She said it aloud under the water, knowing her mother would hear it either way. Merrow swam as fast and as hard as she could, popping her head out of the water to see the soldiers dragging her mother away. They had her mount the back of one of their horses. There were only two men. Merrow realized that she'd been gone longer than she thought because the sun was already lighting up the horizon.

She wanted to help her mother, but was worthless in this form. With a tail, she wouldn't even be able to walk on land. It took time to dry off and for her legs to appear. By then, the soldiers would be back at the castle. Merrow blamed herself that this happened. She never should have asked to go for a swim in the sea. Now, she was about to pay for her mistake.

Her mother looked back at the water as she rode away atop the horse with the guard, talking to Merrow in her mind.

*Find your sisters and take them home, Merrow. Don't come back for me. This is my home now. Save yourselves. Please. Go.*

## Nine

Sebastian awoke early the next morning, having had little sleep. He couldn't stop thinking about Merrow and what she'd said to him. She thought everything he did was because he was looking for approval. She accused him of living his life the way others expected him to instead of how he really wanted. No one had ever said such things before to a king. Didn't she realize he had no choice? He was a ruler and had duties. Responsibilities to fulfill. He had to do whatever it took to protect his people.

"My lord, I can't believe you slept through all the commotion." Hitch ran into the great hall, having come from the courtyard. His men were slowly waking up, but the servants who rose before the sun were already working.

"What are you talking about?" Sebastian asked with a yawn, running his hands over his face. "It is too early for your jabbering, squire." He had a stiff neck from sleeping in his chair while the nymph spent the night in his comfortable, soft bed. He made a face, stretching his neck one way and then the other.

"It's the handmaid you confined to the dungeon,"

said Hitch, talking quickly, being excited about something.

"What about her?" He yawned again and stretched some more.

"The patrol found her by the sea. She escaped and took the gong farmer's wagon to leave."

"What?" He couldn't believe what he was hearing.

"It's true. They're bringing her back to the dungeon though, so don't worry."

"How in the name of Belcoum did she escape? She was under guard. The frail woman is just a simple hand-maid." He sprang to his feet.

"I'm not sure," said Hitch with a shrug. "Mayhap the guards aren't doing their duty."

"Merrow," he said, having a suspicion that she was involved. After all, hadn't she begged him not to put the woman in the dungeon? His action had upset her greatly. He took off at a run with his squire right behind him. Sebastian saw the guard standing watch at his solar door as he came down the corridor. "Did anyone leave that room last night? Answer me," he commanded before the guard could even open his mouth to speak.

"Nay, my king," said the guard with a bow.

"Were you here all night?"

"I replaced the original guard, but there was always someone at this door, my lord."

"Out of my way." Sebastian pushed the guard aside, using the key in his pocket to unlock and push open the door. He bounded into the room to find it empty. "Dammit, she's gone."

"Who's gone?" asked Hitch, looking around the room too.

"The sea nymph." He threw the key down on the bed in anger. "Why do I bother to lock the door when she can pick a lock? What is the matter with me?"

"Don't be so hard on yourself, my lord," said Hitch. "Besides, she's only a sea nymph. What does it matter if she's escaped?"

"Did the watch patrol find anyone with the handmaid?" he asked Hitch.

"Nay."

"Did they question the woman as to if anyone was with her?" He fired questions at his squire one after another.

"I don't know, my king. Would you like me to find out?"

"Nay," he said, slipping his hand into the pouch and fingering her shell charm. "I know where she is, and I'm afraid I don't like it."

"Where is she, my lord?"

"She's gone to Evandorm Castle to get her sisters." Sebastian headed back to talk to the guard at the door. "Fetch Farrimond, quickly," he told the guard. "Tell him I want the army to head out at once."

"My lord?" asked the guard. "They were planning on leaving this morning."

"Well, I want to leave now. Let them know that the king has declared a battle, and it is against those pesky Blackseed brothers who stole the title of king."

* * *

Merrow drove the wagon over the bridge and stopped right outside the gate of Evandorm.

"Who goes there?" called a guard from the battlements, looking down at her. Her head was covered with an old ratty blanket she'd found in the cart so she could hide the hood of Sebastian's robe. She was deciding whether or not to tell them who she was when the guard called down to her again. "Never mind. I can see it's the gong farmer. Open the gate," he told his friends.

Merrow didn't correct him. At least this gained her passage inside. Still, she didn't know why she felt like an intruder. After all, she had done nothing wrong. Merrow figured her best move would be to find her sisters and leave before Sebastian showed up with his army and a battle broke out.

Stopping the cart, she used her mind to call to her sisters. *Melite? Galene? Where are you? I'm here to rescue you.*

*Merrow? We're in the ladies solar next to the great hall.* It was Galene who answered her.

*Hurry, come out to the courtyard. I have a wagon and we need to leave at once,* she told them.

*Nay, not yet, Merrow,* came Melite's voice in her head next. *There is something I need to finish first. Come inside. Please.*

Not understanding why her sisters were acting this way, Merrow got down from the wagon and made her way toward the keep. With the blanket still covering Sebastian's large hood that was hanging over her eyes, she couldn't see well and bumped right into someone. "Oh, I'm sorry," she said, the blanket slipping off and to the ground. Merrow looked up to see a beautiful woman with strawberry-blonde hair and pointy ears, smiling at her. She wore a crown on her head and Merrow realized she must be the queen of the castle. "My lady," she said, attempting a curtsy. Her feet got tangled up in Sebastian's robe. Since she'd just come from the water and her legs were still not that sturdy, she stumbled and fell.

"My goodness. Are you all right?" The kind woman held out her hand to help her up. "I'm sorry, but I don't know you. I am Queen Lira. Who might you be?"

"You're the Elven Queen," Merrow spoke her thoughts aloud without even realizing that she had.

"That's right. And I feel I am at a disadvantage because I still don't know your name." The woman was so nice. She smiled the entire time.

"I'm—Merrow Havfine," looking up. Their eyes met but the woman didn't react. She obviously didn't know she was a sea nymph.

"Welcome to Evandorm Castle, Merrow Havfine. Was there somewhere you were going?"

"I was to meet someone. In the ladies solar."

"Well, let me show you the way."

"Thank you." Merrow silently walked behind the queen, stopping only when they approached the solar door. "It's right here," she said, actually opening the door, even though she was a noble and Merrow was not. "Come inside. We have a sewing circle going on and you are welcome to join us."

"Me? But you don't even know me. I'm no one. Why would you invite me?"

"Because, I can tell by the color of your blue-green eyes that you, my dear, are a sea nymph like Melite and Galene. Am I right?" She raised a brow.

"You are correct." Merrow let out a sigh. "Melite and Galene are my sisters." She lowered the hood to expose her identity.

"Merrow! Look at this." Melite held up a lady's gown. "I sewed it myself. It's so fun. You should try it."

"It seems as if Merrow already has a gown," remarked Galene, looking up from her sewing. "How lucky are you. Did you sew it yourself?"

Merrow stood in shock, barely able to believe these were her sisters. Why were they acting more like humans than undines? Had these humans at the castle changed her sisters this drastically in such a short time?

"What is the matter with you?" Merrow hurried

into the room and walked right up to them. There were several other ladies in the room with them. "We are undines, not humans," she reminded her sisters. "Now put that down. We don't sew." She grabbed Melite's gown, but her sister wouldn't release it.

"Nay, Merrow. Leave it alone. I chose the color pink to go with my new shell necklace. Let go, you're going to rip it."

"Galene? What are you doing?" asked Merrow, hoping since Galene was older than Melite that she'd have more common sense.

"It is actually quite enjoyable, Merrow." Galene pulled the needle and thread through the cloth. "I find it relaxing. You really should try it."

"I will do no such thing! We are sea nymphs and need to get back to the water. Back home!"

"All three of you are welcome to stay for as long as you'd like," offered Lira.

A small lady with chestnut-colored hair and a pixie-like composure ran over with two women who had long, dark hair.

"Hello, Merrow. I am Talia. Darium Blackseed is my husband."

"And I'm Medea, married to Darium's brother, Rhys," said one of the dark-haired women.

"My name is Persimmon," said the third. "My husband is Stone."

"Nice to meet all of you." Merrow nodded, not knowing if she should curtsy or not. She didn't want to be rude since these women all seemed so friendly.

"Everyone is enjoying having your sisters here," Medea assured her. "We wish you would stay as well. Our visit has been so pleasant."

"You might rethink that once you find out that a battle is about to start because of all this." Merrow thought she heard noise out in the courtyard. There was lots of shouting, and the sound of horses' hoofbeats against the cobbled stone.

"What?" gasped Lira. "What do you mean?"

"King Ravenwolf and his soldiers are arriving right now. They plan to steal my sisters and to start a war over it," Merrow relayed the information.

"Nay! Please tell us that isn't so." Lira ran to the window and threw open the shutters. Merrow followed. Sure enough, she could see Sebastian and his army already at the castle's gate.

"She's not lying," said Lira, sounding concerned. "Medea, come with me. We need to stop this."

"I'm glad our husbands all decided to stay here overnight," commented Persimmon. "I feel as if I should have known this was coming. I should have used my crystal ball to scry."

"This is all so sudden," remarked Talia. "I will call to the animals to help us as well."

"Talia, summon Murk. Have him give a message to Zann's mother that her elemental skills are needed."

"Murk?" asked Merrow, confused by all the names of people she'd just met.

"Murk is my husband's raven," explained Talia, approaching the window. "I can speak to animals."

"So, you have magical powers?" Merrow felt excited to learn more about them.

"Yes. We all do," Medea told her. "Persimmon and I are witches, Talia is a fae, and Lira has elven powers."

"So, then you will use your powers against Sebastian and his men?"

"Of course," said Medea. "They can't beat us. Plus, our husbands all have powers too. If King Sebastian and his army want a war, they'll get one. They will regret it when they all end up dead."

"Nay!" shouted Merrow, not wanting Sebastian to die. "There must be another way."

"It's too late." Persimmon spoke over her shoulder, watching out the window. "The Blackseed brothers are confronting King Ravenwolf and his men now. There is no stopping this battle."

"Melite, Galene, you need to help me." Merrow tore the gowns out of their hands and pulled her sisters to their feet. They wore simple long tunics, like the one that Merrow first wore before Sebastian gave her the gown.

"Merrow, what can we possibly do?" asked Galene. "We don't have powers."

"That's right," agreed Melite. "And we are not at an advantage being landbound."

"Come with me," she instructed, taking her sisters each by the hand and running to the drawbridge.

*Ten*

"Why am I not surprised to see her already here?" Sebastian looked over the heads of the Blackseed brothers while talking to his squire, noticing Merrow in the courtyard of Evandorm Castle.

"It's Merrow, my lord," said Hitch, even though everyone could see her for themselves. "That means the Blackseeds have already won. They've captured her."

"Nay, I won't allow it. Over my dead body." Sebastian drew his sword. His army took their cues from him and did the same.

"What is it you want, Ravenwolf?" Zann called out. "You can't come to my gates with your army and weapons drawn and think I'll do nothing about it. Guards, arm yourselves," Zann called out to his soldiers. They ran over and formed a circle around Zann and his brothers.

"Zann, hold up," Rhys warned him under his breath. "We have women and children in the courtyard."

"Everyone get inside for your own safety," was Zann's order. "All soldiers, draw your swords. Be prepared for battle."

"Nay!" shouted Merrow, running forward, pushing her way through the sea of armed men until she got to Sebastian. The magical ladies of the castle were right behind her.

"Medea, get inside," growled Rhys.

"Husband, you know it is really the women who have the magical powers needed to win a war," Medea spoke freely, not sounding at all concerned about offending her husband or the other men. Sebastian found that odd as well as disrespectful.

"No one is going to battle or go to war over me or my sisters," said Merrow.

"Is that what this is all about? The sea nymphs?" asked Darium. He had yet to draw his large blade that was strapped to his back, although it seemed evident a fight was about to break out.

"I want all the sea nymphs. Now, hand them over to me," commanded Sebastian.

"We will not," spat Zann. "Now leave."

"Why would I leave when you have something of mine?" Sebastian looked right at Merrow. "Come, Merrow. I want you back at Macada Castle."

"She's not yours!" Medea's hand swished through the air, causing Sebastian's sword to fly out of his grip. It clattered to the ground. "None of these women belong to any of you."

"That is a definite act of aggression for which you will all pay." Sebastian's eyes turned and he glared at Merrow. She felt his anger and realized he was about to give the command to fight. She also realized that if a fight broke out, Sebastian and his men had no chance of surviving with all the powers these magical beings held.

"You are not taking any of the sea nymphs, Ravenwolf. They are under the protection of me and my brothers," stated Darium.

"That's right," added Rhys. "So, just turn around right now and leave and no one will get hurt."

"I can't do that, Blackseed. And neither will I," Sebastian answered.

Merrow watched in fear as the threat of a battle surfaced. There was no doubt that Sebastian's pride was going to make him order his men to stay and fight, and she didn't like that a bit.

"Wait!" cried out Merrow, bending down to retrieve Sebastian's sword. She picked it up and handed it to him hilt first. "I will return to Macada Castle with you," she told Sebastian.

*Nay, Merrow. What are you doing?* came Galene's silent words in her mind.

*You can't leave us. Please, don't go,* came Melite's silent cry next.

*It's all right. Trust me,* she answered her sisters with her mind. *I don't want anyone to get killed. This is best for now. Meet me at the waterfall at first light. I hear the falls are positioned between all the castles. Just head for the mountains to find them.*

"Let me make sure I understand this. You are volunteering to return with me? On your own?" asked Sebastian.

"Yes. That is correct," she answered.

"Why?"

"I do it with one request only," she told him. "That you and your army leave here now and that no battle breaks happens."

"Well, I'm not sure I like those terms," said Sebastian with a chuckle. "After all, I haven't got everything I came for yet. So tell me, why would I leave?"

"That's right," snarled his captain of the guard from

next to him. "Our king will have everything he wants. As well as all the power."

"Power isn't something that can be given or even stolen," said Merrow, trying to bring peace to this hostile situation. "Like respect, it goes hand in hand along with honor. It is something inborn, not created."

"That's nonsense, my king." Farrimond was ready for a fight and getting the army riled. "The Blackseed brothers stole their kingdoms. Kingdoms that should never be in their hands. Let us fight, my lord. We'll take back all that is rightfully yours."

"Fighting isn't the answer," said Merrow, still holding out his offered sword. "Please," she said in a mere whisper. "Do what you know in your heart is the right thing to do. Even if it is not what's expected of you."


Sebastian scanned the faces of the army of men in Evandorm, weapons drawn, ready to take him down. He took in the frightened looks of Merrow's sisters as they clung to each other, anxiously awaiting his answer. Their eyes were opened wide in fright. Then he glanced over his shoulder at his men. They were ready to do as commanded, but only Farrimond had that hungry look in his eyes wanting to draw first blood.

Was it really fair to his men to make them fight, just to claim a few more sea nymphs? He didn't even know what he'd do with them any of them. The one alone was more than enough trouble as it was. Then again, he was king. Backing down would make him look weak. He couldn't have that. But neither did he want spilled blood over something he couldn't really justify fighting over.

"You'll come with me and not sneak out and leave again behind my back?" asked Sebastian.

"I promise. If you leave my sisters be, I will go with you of my own free will and not try to escape again."

His hand went to his pouch that held her shell charm. He didn't need to make deals with a sea nymph. If he wanted to, he could just control her by using the charm. She would have to heed to his command then. He could still have her, fight his war, and steal the other sea nymphs if he could manage to pull this off. Then again, these beings were all magical. Honestly, his man-power couldn't go up against what they could do without even touching a one of them. He'd seen their effects of magic before. He'd also seen what type of damage could be done. The previous kings of Mura were dead, having lost their lives because magic was involved. Mayhap he should just take the nymph and leave and not look back. Perhaps that would be the best deal of them all.

"I'll call off my men and leave. For now." Sebastian reached out and took his sword from Merrow, sheathing it. "Lower your weapons, men."

Many disappointed grunts and groans filled the air.

"My men, lower your blades as well," Zann called out to his soldiers.

"I will leave with Merrow only," Sebastian said, reaching down and pulling her up atop his horse with him. "However, if any of you come to my door unin-vited again, or try to cause trouble, next time there will be a battle and I will not change my mind about it." He turned his horse as Merrow slipped her arms around his waist to hold on. "I promise you, that battle will not be called off again, because the next one will be a fight to the death."

* * *

Merrow didn't say a word to Sebastian on the way back to Macada Castle. She was too distraught since she kept hearing her sisters calling to her in her mind. Nothing was going as planned. Her hope to rescue her sisters and return home had failed since Sebastian arrived too soon. Or mayhap it was really because she stayed in the ocean too long. Even if she had gotten to Evandorm in plenty of time, did it really matter? Her sisters, for some odd reason, seemed to like living like humans. It sounded to her as if they were in no hurry to get back home. Merrow was afraid that being around these humans was tainting her sisters' minds. Humans and magical beings both, actually. Mayhap that was what made Melite and Galene act this way.

It was up to her now to convince them to go home where they belonged. She kept thinking of her poor mother and how unhappy she seemed to be ever since she turned human. Was giving up everything they loved just to gain a soul worth it? She didn't think so. Merrow had lived for the last one hundred and fifty years as a sea nymph, an undine, and that is how she would someday die. There was nothing here for her on Mura. She needed to find a way to escape again, and this time meet up with her brother who could lead them back through the portal and to their father where they belonged. The hardest part about this plan was that she had no idea how to save her mother, and the last thing she wanted was to leave her behind.

"Why are you so quiet, Merrow?" asked Sebastian.

"I have nothing to say to you," she answered with a sniff. "You tried to control me with my charm to do what you wanted me to do. Then you tried to kidnap my sisters. Plus, you also threw Dee into prison again. You are a horrible, horrible man, Sebastian Ravenwolf!"

He chuckled. "For not having anything to say to me, you certainly managed to convey a lot."

"Well, now I am done." She'd been holding on to him around his waist, sitting behind him atop his steed. But now she released him, not wanting to feel the warmth of his body pressed up against her anymore. Any emotions she had felt for this man were not real, she reminded herself. They were only because he forced them to happen. It was what he wanted, not her.

"Farrimond, take the men back to Macada and wait for me there," ordered Sebastian.

"My lord?" asked Farrimond in surprise. "Where are you going? Not back to confront the Blackseed brothers, I hope. If so, we will accompany you."

"Nay, I assure you I have no plans to go back there. Not yet. Just do what I say. And tell my steward if I am not back by nightfall to serve the meal without me and be sure to close the gate."

"Aye, my king." Farrimond rode to the front of the traveling party while Sebastian directed his horse down a path that led in a completely different direction.

"Where are you taking me?" Merrow demanded to know. "And why did it sound as if we won't return to the castle tonight?"

"I am taking you to a place that I believe will do you good. I am sure you will feel comfortable there."

"I doubt it. Unless you plan on taking me home." She noticed he neglected to mention staying anywhere for the night.

"Home?" he questioned. "Nay. Not exactly. But it's the closest I can do for now so I hope it will suffice." He rode out into a clearing. There before them was a big, tall waterfall with a small lake at the base of it. The water gushed over the rocks, coming from the high mountains above. The sound of the power behind the water and the churning of the falls was like music to her ears.

"It's beautiful!" she exclaimed, her eyes fixed on the lush, green vegetation surrounding the falls. A rainbow of colors danced in the spray of the water as it rushed over the cliff. The roar of strength and nature filled her ears. This flowing water made her feel alive and awakened her senses. "Oh, look at the cute little lily pads and the bright colorful flowers floating on the water."

She couldn't wait to see them closer. Without waiting for Sebastian to help her dismount, she slid off the horse and took off at a run for the lake.

"I thought that might interest you." He tied the horse's reins to a tree and followed her. "This is fresh water, not salt water. Will that make a difference when you submerge yourself in it?"

"What?" Her head snapped around. "What are you saying? You want me to swim in it?"

"Sure. Why not?" he asked with a shrug, sitting atop a nearby rock. "Isn't that what sea nymphs like to do?" He picked up a handful of small stones and one after another started tossing them into the water. Each hit the surface, creating small circles that rippled out wider and wider until they disappeared.

"Well, yes," she admitted. "It is exactly what we like to do." The sounds, the scents of the falls and the lake and the life beneath the surface called to her, begging her to dip her toes into the water. Calling her to go for a swim. She found herself curious as to what underwater life this fresh water lake of Mura held. The beauty of it at the surface alone was intoxicating. What kind of treasures and secrets did it hide?

"What are you waiting for?" The stones he'd thrown were gone now and he brushed his hands together to remove the dirt. "Go for a swim. That's why we're here."

"Oh," she said, knowing that as soon as she touched the water her tail would emerge, as well as her webbed fingers and toes and the fins at the ends of her ears. She would be in her most natural form which meant she'd look and act quite different from Sebastian and the other humans. For some reason, it made her a little nervous. "Mayhap we should return to the castle after all." Feeling emotional about turning back into a sea nymph in front of him, as much as it saddened her, she figured it was best not to do so right now. This was a lake, not the ocean. She'd put herself in a vulnerable position right now to lose her legs. She would be a prisoner again but this time of the small lake since she would not able to swim away. It wasn't at all like being in an ocean. Merrow would also not be able to run away on land if they should be attacked.

"Don't be silly," he said. "The water is refreshing. I know, because I swim here quite often myself when I need to be alone to think."

"Really?" she asked. Hearing him say this, the swim did not seem as threatening to her now. "So...you will be swimming with me?"

"I hadn't planned on it, but why not?" He got off the rock and started to undress.

"What are you doing?" she gasped.

"Well, I can't very well go for a dip with my weapon belt attached and my boots and clothes on, can I?"

"I suppose not."

He detached the pouch he'd had tied to his waist, pausing for a minute, running his hand over it. A shiver ran up her spine. It was the pouch with her charm in it. Was he planning on using it to control her here? She hoped not and wouldn't like that.

"You'd better hurry, or I'm going to be the first one in the water." He gently placed the pouch atop a rock that also held his clothes and weapons. Before she knew it, he stood there in just his braies. So much of his skin showed, that he might as well have been naked. The sun danced on his toned body and illuminated his long, dark hair. His chest was wide and looked very solid. The muscle in his arms and upper body made him look quite strong. He was a true warrior, she could see that.

He noticed her watching him. He grinned and reached for the string holding his braies in place.

"Nay!" She quickly turned and headed for the water. The thought of him standing there stark naked made her mind run in several directions at once. She needed to submerge herself in the cool water to clear her head. Because right now she felt very hot and couldn't stop thinking about them 'almost' having made love.

Wasting no more time, Merrow kicked off her shoes and slipped out of her gown and let it fall, pooling around her feet. She didn't dare look back at him when she heard a splash, knowing he had jumped into the water, and was most likely naked. Pulling her shift up and over her head, she sank down into the cool, fresh water, feeling her change in action. It took only a mere minute or two before her tail emerged and she was a true sea nymph once again.

"Yes!" she said happily, diving down and letting her tail flip up and out of the water. It felt so freeing, so right. This was exactly what she needed right now. This made her happy.

Sebastian dove into the small lake, able to see Merrow underneath the water as her change came about. It was amazing. He had thought he'd always despised magic, since that was what he'd learned from his late uncle. Magic was bad. It was evil. That was what he'd been taught. But seeing the way Merrow transformed from a human into half-fish was something he'd never thought he'd witness. The sunlight streamed through the water and lit up her iridescent tail that magically appeared. Gone were the legs that had made her landbound. Erased was the image of a purely physical girl. She was an undine now. A true goddess of the water. Merrow's smile told him he was right in bringing her here. He held his breath watching her hold out her hands to caress a passing fish. She seemed to honor each underwater creature, and even treat the seaweed as if it were a beautiful bouquet of flowers.

Merrow suddenly realized he was watching her under the surface. She smiled and swam right toward him. Such beautiful curves of her hips and her breasts. Gliding through the water, her long, strong tail propelled her forward effortlessly. It was all muscle and when it moved, it was once of the sexiest things he'd ever seen in his life. Merrow looked elated to be in any underwater paradise, no matter how small.

Sebastian was just about out of air and needed to resurface. He started to swim upward, but she grabbed his arm and held him down. Warning rushed through him. Was she purposely trying to drown him? Was this her plan to make him pay for taking her away from her sisters and keeping her from her true home?

*Relax. Trust me.* He heard her words in his mind and didn't understand how he was hearing her thoughts. It made no sense. Then, he realized what she was doing when she put her mouth up to his and gave him the breath of life, the same as he did for her when she could not breathe after drinking the strong whisky. *Come with me* he heard her words again, even though she hadn't even moved her mouth to speak. They swam together under the water as she pointed out things that Sebastian had never known existed.

*Look* came her thoughts into his head again as she turned over a rock. He discovered a brightly colored salamander dart out and swim up to the surface. Two more overturned rocks led them to a good dozen crayfish. Then she pointed to a turtle swimming by, taking his hand and guiding him to pet its back. Next, she nodded toward a blue frog, swimming after it and following it to the surface. He quickly followed.

When Sebastian popped his head out of the water, he felt invigorated and totally alive. The blue frog hopped atop one of the lily pads. The large pink and yellow flowers that floated on the water gave off a sweet scent that filled the air.

"I never knew there was such beauty under the water," he said, smoothing back his wet hair.

"Yes, there is quite a bit of beautiful underwater life on Mura."

"I agree," he said, drinking in her—the most beautiful water creature of all by far. "Thank you for the breath to allow me to stay underneath the water longer and to see so much more."

"I wanted you to share what I was experiencing." She sank back down, only half her face sticking out of the water now.

"Merrow, something odd happened down there. I heard what you said to me. In my mind."

"Yes." She raised up out of the water to her waist, using her webbed hands to tread water. "Undines are able to communicate by mind alone." She looked even more beautiful in her mermaid form than she did as a human. She wasn't naked, but her aquatic clothes clung to her, showing off her breasts and cleavage. It was almost more like a second skin, or scales, instead of clothes. It looked like a shell of a turtle covering one breast. The other breast wasn't quite as covered.

"But I am not an undine," he pointed out. "Why could I hear your thoughts?"

"It is because you are the holder of my charm. That is why you could hear me."

"Your charm. You mean the shell that fell out of your hair, right?"

"Aye." They floated back over to the shore as they spoke to each other. "When an undine reaches one hundred years of age, she is allowed to acquire a personal charm. This can be anything from a shell to a rock or even a feather, but it is usually a shell from the Mystic Reef."

"Is it hard to find one?"

"Nay. It is something that presents itself to the undine when the time is right. All sea nymphs of age have one and wear it on them at all times. It is best when worn woven into our hair. It becomes part of us, I guess you can say. It holds our thoughts, feelings, emotions, and as you've seen our sexual desires. It is a way for us to control ourselves since sea nymphs have extremely strong feelings, emotions, and of course...sexual desires. Our charm watches over us and keeps us balanced."

"I see." He hoisted himself up out of the water, sitting on the bank with his legs dangling in the lake. He didn't miss the fact that her gaze went straight to his waist. He still wore his braies, not wanting to make her uncomfortable by removing all of his clothing to swim, like he usually did. "So,why is the holder of your charm able to control you? I don't understand that part."

"It only happens when a human is holder of our charm, and something that we hope never happens."

"Why just humans?"

She looked as if she was not going to explain, but changed her mind. She hoisted herself out of the water and plopped down next to him, letting her long tail dip into the water, swishing back and forth as she explained more.

"With so many sisters, every one of us feels our own calling and has a need to explore our own life. Some of us choose to leave the others and move on. A few of my sisters in the past have even ended up choosing to marry humans, and have gained souls, but also become land-bound. Forever. It is a hard decision to make, and often a marriage between an undine and a human does not work out."

"What do you mean? What happens if it doesn't work out?"

"If a human man is married to an undine and he is disloyal to her, either the human man or the undine he married will die."

"Well which is it?" This kind of talk made him feel very uncomfortable since he'd been having all kinds of thoughts regarding her.

"No one knows," she told him. "So far, no human has been disloyal to his undine wife, and we hope to keep it that way."

"Is that so?" He kicked his feet in the water, not knowing what to say to that. "I already saw you have the ability to bring forth legs, but is a marriage between a human and a sea nymph even possible?"

"It's not common, but is very possible, of course."

He found himself curious and needing to know more. "After seeing the beauty of underwater life, why would a sea nymph ever want to live on land?"

"Sebastian, it happens," she told him, twirling the end of a strand of her long hair in her fingers. "It is called falling in love. However, once the decision is made, it can never be reversed. The undine will never be anything but a human from then on."

"I'll bet that is quite a hard decision to make."

"It is a chance that is taken, because by marrying a human, as I've already told you, ensures that the undine will gain a soul."

"It seems like a big sacrifice to make just to get a soul. But I suppose it is an undine's free will to choose that life if she so wishes."

"Some don't have that choice. It is made for them."

"How so?"

"Someone close to me has had her personal charm stolen by a human. He forced her to marry him, even though she was already married to someone else. She turned human and will never again be able to go home to the sea or to the man she loved."

"That's awful. What kind of an ogre would do such a horrible thing?" He reached out and gently placed his hand on her tail, where her leg would be. Her skin felt smooth and soft. He ran his fingers up and down, liking that he was touching her in her sea nymph form.

"That awful man was no other than your uncle, King Leofric Sethor."

"What?" He pulled back his hand and shook his head. "Nay. That makes no sense at all. My uncle never married an undine. He had a human wife."

"Your uncle kept it a secret since he was also married to someone else at the time. This sea nymph I speak of ended up as his prisoner when she fell through a portal and landed in Mura. Sound familiar?"

He knew she was speaking about them now, but chose to ignore that comment. "Who is she? What is your friend's name? I don't think I know her. And where is she now?"

"Her name is Doris," she told him.

"Doris? I don't remember anyone by that name." He thought hard but honestly couldn't remember any woman at Macada Castle or even on Mura named Doris.

"Of course, not. Because your uncle disguised her as a handmaid and her name was changed to Dee. You put her in the dungeon. Twice now."

"Dee? Your handmaid?" he asked in shock, now understanding why she'd been so upset when he'd imprisoned the woman for her bad behavior.

"Yes, Sebastian. That is she. Dee was a prisoner of your uncle and is now your prisoner as well. It seems you are truly following in your uncle's footsteps."

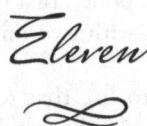

# Eleven

"Oh, Merrow, why didn't you tell me this before now?" Sebastian put his arm around her shoulders, pulling her against his chest. "If I had known—"

"Would you really have done anything different if I had told you?" she asked. "You said you needed to put her in the dungeon to punish her for speaking so boldly to you. You told me that it was expected of you since you were king. And that you didn't want your people disappointed in you."

"Now, in all fairness, I never said that last part."

"Mayhap not, but I know it's what you thought."

"Perhaps I did. Can you ever forgive me?"

"Dee didn't deserve that," she told him. "She is a gentle, kind person who never hurt anyone or anything."

"You're right. I see that now. I promise you, I will release her from the dungeon upon our return."

"You will?" She looked up at him with big, sad eyes. The sunlight lit up her clear blue-green orbs, drawing him in until he felt he would drown in her beauty.

"Yes. I will. For you." He took her hand and kissed her webbed fingers. The sun was starting to dry their

121

bodies, and her hand shifted in his grasp. Magically she had human features now from the waist up but still the tail of a mermaid, being half in the water. He reached over and collected the pouch that held her personal shell charm. Lifting it out with two fingers, he held it up in the sunlight.

"Are you going to use that to control me again?" Her gaze fell to the shell in his hand.

"Nay, Merrow, I'm not. But I am going to give it back to you."

"Y—you are?" She batted away a few tears that welled in her eyes.

"I want you to be in control of your own life and emotions. I want you to be able to make the choice of who you will bed, what you will do, and where you will go. I don't want what happened to Dee to happen to you. No one deserves that."

"So you are setting me free?" she asked, sounding even more shocked than he for what he just did.

"I am," he said, kissing her gently on the hand, still staring into her eyes. He wasn't sure how he was going to explain this action, or his decision to release a prisoner to his advisor and captain of the guard. Neither did it matter right now. He didn't care what others thought of him right now. All he cared about was Merrow and her happiness. He handed her the charm. With trembling fingers she took what he offered. She tied it back into her hair, the shell hanging down in front of one partially exposed breast.

"What will your subjects think of you for this? Won't this action be frowned upon, and make you look like a weak king?" she asked him.

"Aren't you the one who told me not to worry about what others think and to make decisions for myself? Not because it is expected of me?"

"Yes. Yes, I did say that." When her gaze drifted down to his mouth, he thought she wanted to kiss him. Still, he didn't want to misread her and needed to be certain that it was her decision, not his.

"Merrow, there is one thing I will regret by having given you back your personal charm."

"What's that?" she asked, their bodies and faces still close together.

"If I still held the charm, I would know right now exactly what you are thinking." His eyes focused on her lips. He wanted more than anything to kiss her right now.

"Perhaps I can help you know the answer to that." She leaned in closer and kissed him. His heart soared. He hadn't read her wrong after all. The kiss was proper and gentle. He liked it, but found himself wanting so much more.

"I suppose you will be leaving me now? Heading back to your sisters, or to the sea?"

"Nay. Not yet." She smiled as if she knew a secret.

He chuckled because she looked so cute. "What is it?" he asked. "Why don't you want to leave?"

"I heard you tell Farrimond not to wait supper for you. And to close the gate if you don't return tonight. Why did you say that?"

"I guess I was hoping to spend the night with you in my arms. I see that it was too bold to have such hope that it would really happen on its own."

"Was it?" she asked, looking around. "Where did you plan on spending the night?"

"There is a cave behind the waterfall," he told her. "It is private and no one ever goes there. The floor of the cave is covered with soft moss."

"Would you show it to me?" she asked, surprising him once again.

"I will carry you there in my arms if you'd like me to."

"Nay. I will swim while you collect our clothes. I will meet you there." Her smile was infectious, making him smile now as well. She slid back into the water and with a flip of that mighty tail, she disappeared into her underwater world once again.

* * *

With Merrow's shell charm back, she felt invigorated and was no longer under the control of a human man. She'd been sure Sebastian was planning on keeping her charm to control her and get what he wanted. But to her surprise, he suddenly changed from being an ogre to having a heart. He had even brought her to the water, knowing that a sea nymph needed this more than anything else. Such kindness gave her hope for all humans, not just him.

The backside of the waterfall was private, just like Sebastian said it would be. She made it there before him, hoisting herself out of the water, waiting to dry and turn into her human form once again.

"My, you are a fast swimmer." He appeared behind the waterfall carrying their clothes as well as his weapon belt.

"You have no idea what you say. Take me to the sea and I will show you just how fast I really am."

He put down the clothes and walked over to her, reaching down and picking her up in his arms.

"What are you doing?"

"I am helping you get inside the cave."

"I can walk there myself."

"Can you?" He nodded at her tail.

"Well, as soon as I dry off I can."

"Mayhap, I am not willing to wait that long." He carried her inside the cave, laying her atop a patch of soft, green moss.

"Oh, I see what you mean about this patch of moss. It truly is soft. Almost like a bed." She ran her hand over the amazing surface.

"Not quite a bed, but it will do." He went back to retrieve their things, putting them down and sitting next to her. "Are you cold?"

She shook her head. "Undines are used to the cold water. What about you?"

"I am not immune to the cold, however, I can think of a way to warm up quickly." He sat down next to her.

"What would that be?" she asked playfully, knowing exactly what he meant. It was something she was truly looking forward to because she couldn't wait to be intimate with him again.

He kissed her then, and this time ran his hand up and down her tail, caressing her in the most amazing way. Her senses as an undine were heightened. His touch pleased her immensely.

"I like that," she whispered against his lips. "It feels nice."

"What exactly does it feel like to you? I want to know."

She could only think of one thing to explain, and it was to make him feel the same way. "I suppose it feels something like this." She used her hand to rub her fingers up and down his manhood, getting a rise out of him. Instantly, he became hard.

"Oh, I doubt it feels exactly like that," he said, sounding ever so sexy. His hand was on her breast next, fondling her and exciting her at the same time.

"How do I remove this?" he whispered, speaking

about her bodice. He nuzzled her neck and played with her hair.

"There is no way to remove it. Just like my tail. As soon as I dry off, they will magically disappear."

"I'm not sure I can wait that long." He laid her back, straddling her body with his, but holding himself up by his elbows so he wouldn't smash her.

"I think it is working," she said with a giggle. "I am getting very hot now."

He flipped back off of her and tore off his braies, throwing them to the side. She looked down to see his engorged manhood. It was a vision of manly beauty. Merrow couldn't stop herself from reaching down and taking him into both hands. She moaned, coming to life with excitement since sea nymphs had a strong sexual appetite, liking to mate with men of all kinds. She hadn't had one now for fifty years and was hungrier than most her sisters in a situation such as this.

"I think you'd better stop that, or I'll be finished before your legs even appear." He flipped back atop her, straddling his bare legs around her tail, pressing his chest up to hers. "Ooooh, this is a new experience," he said, rubbing his length against her mermaid-type body. "I think I like it."

"I like it too," she admitted, squirming with desire beneath him.

"I hear that sirens of the sea are very lust-filled creatures."

"Yes, they are, but I am not a siren."

"Oh." He stopped moving.

She smiled and continued. "However, I must say that mermaids, undines, sea nymphs, and the like have very hungry sexual appetites."

"I can see why." He glanced down to her tail. "I

would imagine it would be frustrating not to be able to spread your legs."

When he said that, her body temperature rose so much that she was dry instantly. Her tail disappeared along with her sea nymph clothing and her legs appeared. In this form, she was naked.

"That's better," she said, wrapping her legs around his back, surprising him with her action.

"You're naked," he pointed out.

"Yes. And so are you," she answered. "Isn't that usually the best way to couple?"

"As far as I know, it makes it a lot easier." He kissed her on the mouth, then let his kisses trail lower. Before she knew it, he was fondling one breast, slipping her taut nipple between his lips. He suckled her and used his tongue to arouse her even more. She squealed with delight beneath him, liking it, but feeling too constricted.

"Sebastian. I need you to get off of me."

His hands stilled and she could feel the rapid breathing of his heart against her own chest. "Did I do something to displease you?" he asked, sounding cautious, but genuinely sorry if he had. He also sounded a little scared that she was going to stop their lovemaking before they'd had a chance to find their release.

"Don't worry," she told him with a wink. "It is just that sea nymphs are aggressive during lovemaking and don't like to be constricted by being on the bottom."

"Really?"

"I'll let you be the judge of that." She pushed him to the bed and crawled atop him, spreading her legs around him like she was about to ride a horse. Desire dwelled inside her, and this man had fed that need with his kindness when he brought her to the waterfall, and then gave her back her shell charm. This was a man she was interested in coupling with, not the man he was when she'd first met him. No human man she'd ever heard of had given back a sea nymph's personal charm, hence giving up control over her. No man she'd ever met had changed so much in such a short time. This side of Sebastian Ravenwolf wasn't greedy and evil. This part of him was kind and giving. That was exactly what she wanted in a man but thought she would never see.

She leaned forward and kissed him the same way he had kissed her. Her mouth trailed down his chest and she licked his nipple, causing it to turn to a hard nub. He laughed.

"That tickles," he told her. "Mayhap we'll leave that move to me when I kiss you."

"Whatever you like." She ran her hands up and down his sturdy chest, licking his skin, getting lower and lower. He started to say something to her but stopped when she took his erection into her mouth and pleasured him with her lips and tongue. He squirmed beneath her.

"Merrow, you are driving me mad," came his voice through his heavy breathing.

"You don't like this?" She used her hands to pleasure him more.

"Oh, I like it. Too much. But you need to stop that, because I cannot hold back much longer."

"Oh, you mean to you want to make love the usual way."

"I'm not sure what is usual for a sea nymph, and I am up for trying anything you suggest. However, at the moment, I am ready to explode. Please, let me enter you now."

"Let me help."

Taking him into her body, Merrow felt his warmth and his strength as he filled her completely. His thrusts started out gentle, the touch of his hands against her skin like a feather brushing the surface. This felt right. Merrow moved her hips, the way an undine did to swim, and it seemed to make him squirm even more beneath her.

"Oh, you have no idea what you are doing to me you naughty little sea nymph."

"Do you like it?"

"Do I!"

She liked it too, and that made her happy. There was no harm in spending time together, coupling the way a man and a woman were meant to do.

They did the dance of love, their movements fluid like the water, but their bodies both burning for each other like her special times, bathing in the sun. Something came to life inside her that she'd never felt before. All that mattered in this time, in this very moment was to give this man pleasure and to feel that same pleasure in return. However, this seemed to be going far beyond any of her expectations.

"Merrow, I don't want to hurt you."

"You couldn't hurt me, my lord. I hope I don't hurt you."

That made him chuckle as they continued to kiss while they coupled. He pulled back long enough for her to hear his reply.

"The only way you could possibly hurt me is if I find my release before you experience yours."

"How about we find it together, then?" she asked, feeling her heart about ready to explode, from not lust, but love. All the love she felt for her sisters, her underwater home and the creatures that walked the earth and swam in the sea, was here now within her. She experienced joy, happiness, and a carefree feeling that everything would be all right. Merrow wanted Sebastian to feel this way too. She wanted to feel these emotions together.

Their rhythm picked up and their hips moved faster and faster. She didn't hold back, but moved atop him the same way she did when she moved her hips to swim through the water using her tail to propel her. Their bodies made a slapping noise as they came together. The sound excited both of them. Her heart beat faster, and she noticed his breathing change. So did hers. They were climbing the precipice and about to reach that peak of fulfilled desire. Together.

Sebastian growled loudly like an animal, the sound calling to her in a primal way, until she released screaming noises that she hoped wouldn't scare him off.

She cried out. So did he. Colors exploded behind her closed lids and her senses, since she was a sea nymph, were enhanced more than ever before. She could smell the scent of happiness, taste the flavor of joy. Merrow could feel the overwhelming emotion spilling forth, filling the air all around them. This seemed more than just lust and sexual fulfillment. She felt the two of them come together as if they were part of nature. Part of each other. Like they belonged together. If she didn't know better, she'd say that possibly what she was feeling...was love.

Sated and spent, she rolled off of him, cuddling up and resting her cheek against his bare chest. Breathing hard, he reached out and smoothed down her hair. His hand almost touched her shell charm woven into her locks, but he was careful and pulled his hand away at the last second. If he had touched it, she wasn't sure that it, as well as she, wouldn't shatter in his arms.

"I've never coupled with a sea nymph before," he whispered, kissing her atop the head. "I must say it was exhilarating. After that, I am not sure I will ever be able to couple with a human woman again."

It was meant as a compliment, she was sure, but for some reason his words made her feel empty and sad. Part of her wanted to claim him as hers. She didn't want to share Sebastian with any human woman. But to want that was selfish she supposed. After all, she was about to leave Mura forever and go back home. Sebastian would want a wife and queen here on Mura. He would need a woman who could not only satisfy him, but remind him that he didn't need to care what anyone else thought about him and that he didn't need to listen to anyone's feelings but his own.

Merrow was an undine. She belonged in the Aegean Sea, not the Masked Sea. Her home was with her forty-nine sisters and her brother, not in a castle with armies, living on land, and eating in a great hall. He needed someone who could fill that position. It should be a woman who could serve as queen of Macada Castle, as well as wife to the king. That is, a woman who could bear him as many heirs as he wanted.

She was Merrow Havfine, from a different world, she reminded herself. Just a poor girl who was at the wrong place at the wrong time and was accidentally sucked through a portal. That is what brought her to Mura, and that same portal would take her home now as well.

She could never be the woman that Sebastian needed and wanted.

Nay, never.

Or could she?

# Twelve

M errow awoke during the night, hearing her sisters calling to her in her mind. Still wrapped in Sebastian's arms after their love-making, she hated to go.

*Merrow? Merrow, we're here. Where are you?* She heard her sister, Galene calling to her.

*I will be right there,* she told her sisters in the language of the sea nymphs. She gently removed herself from Sebastian's protective hold, donning her gown and shoes. Then with one last look at her lover, she turned and headed out to the lake from their secluded spot behind the waterfall.

Merrow heard giggling and splashing as soon as she walked out into the open area. Her attention was drawn to the pool of water at the foot of the falls. She saw one tail and then two break the surface. Splashing continued as her sisters played in nymph form diving under the water and breaking the surface again.

"Melite, Galene, what are you doing?" This, she said aloud. The sun was just rising on the horizon and it was the beginning of a new day.

The girls' heads poked up one after the other and they called out to her in true undine fashion.

"Come, sister," begged Melite. "Join us. This water is fine. Let's all play and go for a swim together."

"I've already done that," she told them, memories of yesterday with Sebastian flitting through her mind. "Come out of the water at once. You are wasting precious time. We need to get back to the sea and wait for Nerites."

"Let us play for a while longer," said Melite, sounding sad. "We haven't swum in days now and need to do this. I missed it."

"Did you really?" she asked. "By the look of the two of you sewing gowns in the ladies solar at Evandorm, I'd guess that you didn't miss anything at all about being a sea nymph. Matter of fact, it seemed to me that you liked living like humans."

"The Blackseeds and their family and friends are so nice," Galene told her. "I wish you would have had the chance to get to know them the way we have."

"Don't let every kind human sway your decisions," she warned them, half-wondering if she was really saying this to herself as well.

"How did you get away from the king?" Galene asked her. "I thought he took you back to the castle to imprison you."

"Nay. Sebastian is kind. He didn't do that."

"So he is nice like the Blackseeds?" asked Melite, squirting water from her mouth and holding up a frog as she giggled.

"Yes. I suppose so," she said, not sure how to answer. Merrow realized that the Blackseeds and King Ravenwolf were mortal enemies.

"Then what happened? How did you escape him?" asked Melite.

Merrow couldn't stop herself from thinking about making love with Sebastian. As soon as she thought about it, both her sisters read her mind and knew exactly what had happened between them.

"You made love with a man!" gasped Galene.

"A human man," said Melite looking and sounding so disappointed.

"So what if I did?" she asked. "I am old enough to make that decision for myself."

"Sister, is he controlling you?" asked Melite. "Is he using your charm to make you like him?"

"Nay. Or, not anymore, I should say. He did use it against me at first. However, he gave it back to me. Sebastian didn't control me to convince me to make love with him, I swear. That was all my own decision. See, I have my shell charm back." She picked up the lock of hair that had her personal charm attached to it, showing them that what she said was true.

"Then he won't stop you from leaving with us either," said Galene. "Right?"

"I–I don't think so." She suddenly realized she wasn't sure. He had given her freedom back, but she was still confused as to if he wanted her to leave or stay with him. "I'm actually not sure how he will feel if I leave." Merrow glanced back at the waterfall and her heart ached. Part of her wanted Sebastian to try to stop her from going. To stay with him because he enjoyed her presence in his life. Then again, if he dared try keeping her here and wouldn't let her leave with her sisters, that would make her angry too. Confusion muddled her mind.

"Perhaps we shouldn't wait to find out." Galene hoisted herself up and out of the water. "Come, Melite. We need to dry off so we can gain our legs. There will be no way for us to travel in our sea nymph forms."

"Speaking of that," said Merrow curiously. "How

did you two get here by yourselves? Did you manage to escape and find your way to the falls by luck alone?"

"They're not by themselves. They had a little help."

Merrow turned to see Medea standing there with her husband, Rhys. "You two helped them?" asked Merrow.

"Yes," answered Medea. "Your sisters told us what they wanted to do and I helped them get here. Of course, I could only use my magic to transport them one at a time."

"My brothers and I want to see you and your sisters get back home through the portal," said Rhys.

"Thank you." Merrow smiled and nodded. "However, transporting us one at a time will take too long." She started to feel suddenly panicked. "Sebastian will be awake at any moment. I am not sure he's going to just let us all leave. That might make trouble for him. His men may not respect him and think of him as weak if we just disappear."

"Sister, you are starting to sound like you're making up excuses to stay here," Galene told her.

Mayhap she was, she sadly realized. Everything was happening so fast that she needed time to stop and think things over regarding what happened between her and Sebastian. Mayhap leaving right now wasn't the answer after all.

Someone cleared their throat and everyone turned around to see Elric sitting in a horse-drawn wagon. He was on the driver's seat with the reins in his hand.

"Elric?" asked Merrow. "What are you doing here?"

"I overheard the plan and knew it wouldn't work. That's why I brought the wagon. Get in. Hurry. I will take all of you directly to the sea. Anything to get Mura back to the way it was."

"We can't go anywhere until my sisters have their

legs," Merrow told him. They need to dry off some more first in order for that to happen."

"Well, that's gratitude for you," said the elf with a scowl, mumbling to himself.

"Someone's coming!" Medea looked over at the waterfall.

"It's Sebastian," said Merrow. "He's coming to find me."

"Merrow? Is that you?" Sebastian called out, appearing from behind the falls.

"Sisters, we need to get you into the wagon. Quickly," warned Merrow, seeing Sebastian stop, taking in the situation.

"What's going on here?" he asked. Sebastian was fully dressed and his hand wavered above the hilt of his sword strapped to him.

"We can't leave!" cried Melite. "We still have our tails."

"Don't worry. I'll bring you to the wagon." Medea took Melite's hand and transported her. They disappeared and then reappeared in the back of the wagon.

"Now me," cried Galene. "Please, hurry. I don't want to be trapped here."

"Merrow, as those your sisters? What are they doing here?" Sebastian started toward them at a quick pace. "Wait! Don't leave. You can't."

"Go!" Merrow commanded Medea. Medea took Galene's hand next and transported her to the wagon as well.

"Merrow, hurry!" cried Galene from the cart.

Merrow stood still, not able to move. Part of her wanted to go home with her sisters. Another part of her wanted to stay with Sebastian. She hadn't had time to think things over yet. After last night, nothing was the same. Merrow hadn't even had the chance to tell Sebastian goodbye.

"Merrow, stop! Please. And keep your sisters from leaving," yelled Sebastian, hurrying toward her. "You can't go."

When Merrow heard those words, she realized it was exactly what she had to do. If she didn't try to get her sisters back through the portal now, she might never be able to do it again. She was sure by now her brother would be waiting, and she wasn't sure how long he could keep the portal open.

Merrow turned and ran for the wagon, jumping on the back just as Elric pulled away in a hurry. Medea was with them in the back and Rhys rode up front with the elf.

"Merrow! Merrow, come back." Sebastian shouted, but Merrow didn't answer because she wasn't sure what to say. All she could do was to stare at the man who had been her lover. Her protector. Someone whom she wished she'd had the chance to get to know even better.

"Get to the sea quickly and don't stop, no matter what," Merrow ordered Elric over her shoulder.

Sebastian's image got smaller and smaller as they traveled down the road, leaving him behind. Merrow's heart felt heavier than it ever had before. In her haste, she hadn't thought this through. By going, she wasn't only leaving Sebastian behind, but she'd also just abandoned her mother.

\* \* \*

Sebastian never expected this! He wasn't sure what happened. When they went to sleep last night, he and Merrow were getting along fine. More than fine. They'd held each other and kissed and made love. They'd spent the night together in each other's arms, laughing and talking. They'd been intimate in not only the physical way but also with their thoughts, words and actions. They even shared stories, fears and wants. He had never talked like this and opened himself up this way with any woman before. Then again, Merrow was so much more than just any woman. She was special. Caring. Kind. She was a sea nymph. A true, unique beautiful, loving woman.

And now, this girl who had made him so happy, without even a simple goodbye just rode out of his life. Forever.

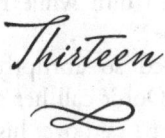

*Thirteen*

"**O**pen the gate," Sebastian shouted, riding up the drawbridge of Macada Castle, not bothering to even slow his horse.

"It's the king!" shouted the lookout atop the battlements. "Quickly, raise the gate."

The gate lifted slowly, squeaking, creaking, and rattling as it enabled him access to his home. Sebastian lowered his head and upper body closer to his horse as he rode through to the courtyard, not even waiting for the gate to lift up all the way.

"My lord!" Farrimond and Drell were in the stable. They saw him and came running across the courtyard with a stableboy right behind them.

"My king, we were concerned when you didn't return last night," Drell told him.

"Farrimond, didn't you give the others my message?" Sebastian slid off his horse feeling frustrated for more than one reason. He tossed the reins to the waiting stableboy.

"Yes. Yes, I did, my king." Farrimond bowed. "I told them to close the gate for the night if you didn't return in time."

"Good." Sebastian nodded and started walking at a brisk pace toward the keep.

"Where is the girl, my lord?" asked Drell, making haste to stay next to him while he walked. "The sea witch. Did she escape?"

Sebastian stopped so abruptly that Drell almost crashed into him. "Don't call her a sea witch again, or I'll have your head," he said over his shoulder, not bothering to look back. He entered the keep and made his way to the great hall. "Jocet! Hitch! Where are you?" He headed over to his chair in front of the fire where he liked to sit and think.

"My king!" Jocet raced out of the kitchen with a metal pitcher of ale in his hand. Hitch hurried after him with the king's ornate tankard, shining it with the sleeve of his tunic as he walked. "We didn't know you'd returned."

"Ale," he commanded, plopping down in his chair.

His steward poured him a tankard and handed it to him.

"Where's the mermaid?" asked Hitch.

Sebastian downed the contents of the cup and held it out for more. "She's not here, squire. I thought that would be obvious, even to someone like you."

"We see that, my lord." Jocet filled his tankard once again. "Is everything all right?"

By this time, his advisor and captain of the guard had joined them.

"Of course, everything is not all right. One of the Blackseed brothers, his wife, and that obnoxious elf not only left with the other two sea nymphs, but with Merrow, too."

"They stole the sea nymph?" asked Drell. "This is awful. How did they get her when she was under your protection?"

"I knew I should have stayed to assist you, my lord." Farrimond shook his head in disgust.

"I don't need assisting or protecting." Sebastian's head ached and his body felt stiff from sleeping on the ground in the cave. "Merrow left of her own accord. It was her choice to go back to the sea. No one stole her from under my nose."

"Her choice? Now you're giving our prisoners a choice?" snapped Drell.

"She wasn't a prisoner," Sebastian corrected him. "Not really."

"I thought you held some kind of control over her," said Farrimond in confusion.

"I did. But I gave her back her shell charm, and had no control over what she did. Or does anymore."

"My king, I advise you to go after her," urged Drell.

"I agree," broke in Farrimond. "I'll ready the army. We can head them off before they make it to the sea. Even against magic, we'll still have the numbers to put up a good fight. I am sure we can get her back, as well as claim her sisters as ours, too." He turned to go get the soldiers, but Sebastian stopped him.

"Nay! They don't belong here, and certainly cannot and will not be owned by any of us. Hearing what you two are saying, I cannot blame them for wanting to leave."

"What are you saying, my lord?" Drell leaned in closer to speak softly in his ear. "If you let them leave, you lose all respect of your men. Not to mention, you'll look like the weakest king that ever ruled Mura."

"Nay. That's not true." Anger grew within him.

"Then prove it, my lord. Take your troops to the sea and bring back what is yours." Drell wouldn't back down and it made Sebastian feel anxious and upset.

Sebastian truly didn't want to look like a weak ruler.

Neither did he want Merrow leaving before she'd even given him an explanation as to why she didn't want to stay. He had to go after her, even if it was only to hear what she had to say. "All right. Prepare the troops, but no one leaves before I am ready." He started to walk away.

"Where are you going, my lord?" called out Drell.

"I have to make a quick trip to the dungeon and then we'll be on our way."

Sebastian hurried to the dungeon, pushing open the door to find his guard eating a meal and drinking wine. "Open the cell door of the handmaid," he instructed.

"Yes, my king." The guard did as ordered.

Sebastian stepped in through the open cell door, stopping when he saw the woman hunkered down in a heap on the floor with her arms wrapped around her. She looked tired and weak and almost as if she were dying. "When is the last time she had food or water?" he asked the guard.

"Yesterday, my lord," answered the man. "Before she escaped."

"Why haven't you given her anything since?"

"I figured you would want her punished, like any of the other prisoners who try to escape."

"Dammit, I never gave that order," he shouted. "Now, go get your food and wine and give it to her. And hurry!"

"Aye, my king." The guard rushed away to do as ordered.

"Dee, get up," he told the woman, walking over and pulling her to her feet. When the woman looked up at him with hollow eyes, he could tell she'd been crying.

"Kill me if you need to, but please don't hurt Merrow," came the woman's plea. "She only helped me escape because she felt she needed to do so, but I am not going anywhere. Please, don't hurt her, my king."

"Merrow has escaped with her sisters and is heading to the sea as we speak."

"She has?" Hope filled her eyes. "Then they have a chance to get back home after all. Thank the gods that they will soon be back through the portal."

"What do you mean she felt as though she needed to help you? Is it because, like she told me, you were once a sea nymph too?"

"Nay, my lord, that is not the reason at all. It is so much more than that. A much deeper reason." She looked directly into his eyes now, all her fear having left when she discovered the sea nymphs were headed back to the sea.

"Then what?" he asked, needing to know. Such devotion between Merrow and this simple handmaid was like nothing he'd ever seen before.

"I suppose it no longer matters if I tell you, my king. Before you can stop them, they'll have made it back to the sea and they will be wary of your nets this time. Once they are in the water and in their undine forms, you'll never be able to catch them."

"Tell me what?" he asked, not understanding any of this. It almost sounded as if the women held some sort of secret between them.

"King Ravenwolf, there is something special between me and Merrow, as well as me and Galene and Melite. You see, I love them all deeply and they love me too."

"You do?" he asked, having felt something that might be love for Merrow as well when they'd spent the night together.

"I do. I love the three of them as well as all the rest of my many children."

"What are you saying? Do you mean that Merrow and her sisters are—"

"Yes, my lord. The sea nymphs are my daughters."

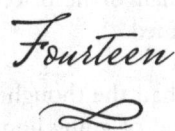

# Fourteen

Merrow's heart ached as they headed for the sea in the back of the wagon. While Melite and Galene were excited to be going back home, she couldn't honestly say she felt the same way.

"What's the matter, sister?" asked Melite. "You look so sad."

"Did something bad happen between you and the king?" asked Galene. "I hope he didn't hurt you."

"Nay, he didn't. Just the opposite," answered Merrow. "You both know what happened."

"Opposite?" asked Medea. She smiled, knowing exactly what she meant. "You made love with King Ravenwolf, didn't you?" asked the witch. "My guess is that you've also fallen in love with him."

"What?" Rhys looked over his shoulder and scowled at having overheard this.

"Yes, you are right. I did make love with him," Merrow admitted, not ashamed of what she did and not caring who knew. "I also have feelings for him, but since I don't know exactly how it feels to be in love I cannot answer your question truthfully."

"Do you think of him constantly?" asked Medea.

"I do," Merrow answered, smiling at the memories she had of him.

"Does your body warm and act all tingly when he brushes back your hair or he places his hand on your arm?" Medea continued.

"Yes. Yes, it does."

"And have you had the thought of mayhap staying here on Mura instead of going home through the portal?" Medea asked the last question.

Merrow hesitated before she answered this one. Looking over at her sisters, she realized she couldn't lie to them because they would only read the truth in her thoughts. "I...I suppose I have fantasized of mayhap staying here in Mura. With Sebastian. Mayhap even as his wife," she admitted.

"Nay! You don't want to marry that oaf," shouted Elric, having been listening to their conversation. "Go back home where you belong. Forget all about the fool. He is not one of the good kings of Mura. He is an evil one."

"Nay. You're wrong," Merrow defended him. "Sebastian might care too much what others think of him, but he is not evil like his uncle."

"How can you say that?" asked Rhys. "You didn't even know King Sethor."

"Nay, but I heard all about him. Sebastian doesn't want to follow in his uncle's footsteps. He doesn't want to be an evil, unforgiving, vengeful king at all."

"If she believes that, then yep, she's in love," scoffed the elf, ending with a big, sad sigh. "We need to get her back through that portal quickly, even if we have to push her through it. She doesn't belong here, and she and her sisters have to go as well. If Merrow stays, she'll only end up like the last one."

"Like the last one?" asked Medea. "Elric, what or who are you talking about?"

"Was there another sea nymph here at one time?" asked Galene curiously.

"There was, and it didn't end up pretty." Elric continued to direct the horse. They were nearing the Masked Sea.

"Sister, what are they talking about?" Melite asked Merrow directly, making her realize she couldn't keep her promise to her mother any longer. Merrow figured that her sisters deserved and needed to know the truth.

"They are talking about Mother," said Merrow, watching her sisters' eyes grow wide.

"Mother was here?" asked Galene.

"I thought she died," said Melite.

"She didn't die," Merrow explained. "She was sucked through the portal, just like us. But the last King of Macada, the evil one, married her."

"Why didn't I know about this?" asked Rhys from the front, seeming as if he felt left out.

Merrow continued. "King Sethor was already married but married our mother as well. In doing so, she gained her soul, but lost her tail and turned human forever."

"Did the king kill her?" asked Melite.

"Where is she now?" Galene wanted to know.

"Mother is alive and at Macada Castle," explained Merrow.

"She is?" her sisters said together.

"Yes. She is."

"Why didn't you tell us, Merrow?" Galene looked so disappointed in her.

"I want to see Mother," whined Melite.

"It was Mother's wish that no one knows about this. Especially not Father," explained Merrow.

"Why not?" asked Medea.

"You don't know our father," said Merrow. "He

would be so angry if he found out, that he would destroy all of Mura in retaliation."

Rhys chuckled. "I don't believe one man could do that much damage. Especially when there are so many of us in Mura who have magic."

"One man couldn't. You are right," said Merrow. "Then again, our father is not a man, and he does have magic."

"Is he a sea nymph. Like the three of you?" asked Medea. "Even so, what real powers do sea nymphs have?"

"Yes, he's a sea nymph, in a way," Merrow answered.

"Back home he is known to everyone as the Old Man of the Sea," added Galene.

"Old? How old is he?" asked Rhys. "I can't imagine an old man fighting against an entire army." He chuckled again.

"Six thousand," said Merrow.

"What?" asked Rhys.

"Our father is six thousand years old." The people in the wagon all became silent.

"Finally, someone older than me," the elf spoke up. "But I'm sure he's not as fast as I am. Especially at his age."

"He can swim at extreme speeds," Merrow told him. "Plus, he can control the water."

"And shapeshift," added Melite. "Don't forget about that."

"He can do all those things?" asked Medea, sounding fascinated. "He's not a witch like me, is he? I can shapeshift too."

"Nay, of course, he is not a witch." It was Merrow's turn to chuckle now. "Our father is a god."

"A god?" said Medea, Elric, and Rhys all together.

"Yes. A sea god," answered Merrow. "And like I told

you, it's not a good thing if he comes through the portal and is angry."

"We'll just hope he never comes through the portal then," Rhys answered. "Hopefully he'll never find out about any of this."

"Too late," mumbled Merrow under her breath.

"Merrow? What does that mean?" asked Medea.

"Our only brother, Nerites was already here on Mura and knows everything about what happened. He has returned home to let our father know where we are."

"Bug's eyes, we're doomed," said Elric in his nasally voice. "There is no way we can fight off a god."

"Medea, transport me back home, immediately," said Rhys.

"Why?" she asked.

"Because, I have a bad feeling about all this. I think we're going to need the help of my brothers."

Merrow watched Rhys and Medea disappear, feeling like a battle was about to begin. She didn't want trouble. The best thing she could do to protect the people of Mura was to get herself and her sisters through the portal and leave this place forever.

"Elric, drive faster," she told the little man. "It is important that I get my sisters back through the portal before my father comes looking for us."

"I'm going as fast as I can with you three along." The elf drove recklessly and before long they stopped at the edge of the sea. "All right. You're here. So go," said the elf, not being one for manners.

"Come, sisters. We need to get into the water. Quickly." Merrow held out her hands to help them exit the wagon.

"All right, but how will we find the portal?" asked Galene.

"And how will we open it again?" asked Melite.

"Nerites will have told Father everything by now, and also returned to open the portal with the Calling Conch," said Merrow. "Now, hurry. If we call to them with our minds, mayhap there doesn't have to be a battle at all. Let's get home."

The girls slipped into the water and shifted back into their sea nymph forms.

"This feels wonderful!" Melite dove down, slapping the water with her tail.

"Merrow, I'm glad you decided to come home with us," Galene said with a look of relief. "For a minute there, I thought you were going to want to stay in Mura with Sebastian."

From the water, Merrow looked back at the shore. The elf was still there. Medea was bringing the Blackseed brothers one at a time, and each of them was armed with weapons.

"These people are nice," Merrow told her sister. "When I saw you and Melite sewing, I honestly thought you both wanted to stay."

"We do like it here," Galene told her. "But it isn't our home, Merrow. We are sea nymphs and belong with our father and our siblings in the Aegean Sea."

"Yes," she agreed, letting out a sigh and looking back to the shore once more, expecting to see Sebastian. Part of her had hoped that he followed and would try to convince her to stay. But he didn't. Perhaps she'd misread his feelings for her after all. Mayhap it was good that he wasn't here. It couldn't work out between them since they were so different. She supposed it was better in the end if Sebastian forgot about her. "What about Mother?" she asked Galene. "Don't you want her home too?"

"I do. Of course, I do," said Galene, treading water with her arms. "But you said Mother didn't want anyone to know her secret."

"I did. I promised her I wouldn't tell anyone. But how long do you really think we can keep this secret from Father?"

"He'll read Melite's mind if nothing else," said Galene. "Our little sister isn't strong enough yet to disguise her thoughts."

"I agree. I never should have left Mother. Galene, I'm going back to find her. I want to take her through the portal with us."

"You won't have to do that you silly sea witch." Elric came riding up on the back of a dolphin, having overheard them yet again. "Your mother as well as King Ravenwolf and his entire army are approaching right now. Find the portal, fast. Get out of here before the battle begins."

"Nay, Elric, I can't do that," said Merrow, seeing Sebastian leading his army to the shore. Her mother rode on the back of the horse with him. "I cannot believe Sebastian has listened to his men, and is going to start a war over this. And even worse, he has brought Mother along with him. I am going to give him a piece of my mind right now."

Just then, Melite and their brother Nerites popped their heads out of the water.

"Merrow, Galene, come quickly," said Melite. "Father has opened the portal using his Calling Conch."

"It won't stay open long," explained Nerites. "Father sent me to get you."

"Brother, take Galene and Melite and go through the portal," said Merrow. "There is something I have to do."

# Fifteen

Sebastian stopped his horse on the shore, able to see Elric in the water atop a dolphin, and several heads that from this distance looked to be the sea nymphs. Merrow included.

"Call to your daughter," Sebastian told Dee, getting off the horse. "Tell her in your mind that I want to talk to her."

"It is dangerous for me to do that," said Dee. "If there are other sea nymphs in the water, they will hear my thoughts."

"So? What is wrong with that?" He reached up and helped her dismount.

"I don't want my husband to hear my thoughts. If so, there will be trouble."

"Your husband is dead," Sebastian reminded her.

"Not that ogre, King Sethor. I mean my real husband, Nereus."

"Who?"

"He is known on the other side of the portal as Old Man of the Sea."

"So, he's an old man, then." Sebastian nodded. "I promise, if he emerges, I won't let my men hurt him."

"Hurt him?" She laughed. "You'd better pray he

155

doesn't come through that portal. Because even though he is six thousand years old, he is more powerful than any or all of your army."

"Six thousand years old?" Sebastian laughed, thinking she was jesting. Then, when he saw the serious look on her face, he knew she wasn't. "All right, just call for Merrow and I'll take it from here."

"She already knows you are here and is calling for you to come to the edge of the water."

"All right. I will," said Sebastian, not feeling threatened in the least. He walked past his army, his captain of the guard stopping him.

"My king, I see the Blackseed brothers here." Farrimond drew his sword, the sound of metal ringing in the air. "Shall I command the men to attack? We could take them out easily since I don't see too many of their magical women with them."

"I agree. Attack right away." Drell rode up on his horse to join them. "It is your big chance to take over their kingdoms. Their armies are not with them and we have a fighting chance. Do it, now."

"Nay! Wait," said Sebastian.

"Whatever for?" asked Drell. "I am your advisor, and I tell you to attack. Your uncle always listened to me, so what is your problem?"

"My uncle is dead," said Sebastian. "So tell me, where did your advice really get him? Now everyone, stay here. Don't approach us, and don't come to the shore unless I command it." He took Dee by the arm and they trudged down to the water's edge together.

"Mother!" Merrow cried out from the water, holding on to a pier.

"Merrow. Daughter!" Dee ran to the water's edge, kicking off her shoes and wading waist deep into the sea to be near her daughter.

"Merrow! I need to talk to you." Sebastian hurried after her. But by the time he got down to the shore, something was happening. The water swirled and huge waves thrashed back and forth. The sea became suddenly rough as if there was a bad squall spat up from nowhere. He looked upward but there wasn't a cloud in the sky. It was the oddest thing he'd ever seen.

"Merrow, come quickly." Melite stuck her head out of the water. "We have a problem."

"What problem?" asked Merrow.

"I'm sorry, but Father read my mind and knows what happened to Mother and that she is here. He is furious. He has just come through the portal and is seeking revenge."

"Oh, no!" Merrow looked back at her mother. "It's happening, Mother. I'm sorry. But a war is about to be fought over this no matter if we like it or not."

"A war? About Sethor marrying Dee?" Sebastian couldn't understand this. "Just explain to him that Sethor is dead. It's over now. There is no one to exact revenge upon."

"He said he's going to kill Sethor's successor," said Nerites, their brother, sticking his head out of the water next.

"This is bad," said Merrow, looking really afraid. "I'm so sorry, Sebastian. It wasn't supposed to end this way."

"End? Sorry? What are you talking about, Merrow? I can fight off one man, don't worry. I can take care of myself."

"Mayhap a man, you could," she told him. "But not my father."

"Because he's a sea nymph?" asked Sebastian. "I hardly think he is dangerous since he can't leave the water."

"Think again," said Dee, nodding at the swirling water before them. Up rose a man with long, white hair and an even longer white beard. His chest was bare. Instead of a tail like the girls, this man had the body of a sea serpent! He was huge. Nereus held a shell-like horn of some kind in one hand and a long pointed three-pronged trident in the other. The end of his tail slapped the water, and it looked like a sharp spike.

"Merrow, this is your father?" he asked in a low, steady voice.

"Yes, Sebastian. It is he."

"I don't know how to fight a...a...sea serpent, or whatever he is."

"He's not a sea serpent, Sebastian." Merrow looked at her father and then back and him. "However, he is shapeshifter, so I would advise you and your army to run."

"Run? I have never run away or backed down from a fight in my life and don't intend to do so now. I will never ask my men to do so either."

"He'll turn into a land creature and hunt you down," said Dee. "Take my daughter's advice. Please, go back to your castle before you are hurt or killed."

"I can fight him, don't worry. Merrow, I promise I will also defend you and your mother and sisters."

"There is no way you can do that, Sebastian," Merrow answered, making him think that she thought of him as less than a king or a man with good fighting skills. What did he have to do to prove to her his worth?

"You don't believe in me, Merrow. That hurts right here." He thumped his balled-up fist against his chest. "I can see that you don't think much of me as a man, a soldier, or a king."

"Stop saying that, Sebastian. It's not true," she cried.

"I wish you would stop caring what others think of you once and for all."

"Well, I had really hoped you'd have feelings for me like I do for you."

"You do?" she asked, her brows arched and a smile slowly spread across her face. "Of course, I have feelings for you, Sebastian. I don't know why you'd even think that I didn't."

"I love you, Merrow, and came down here today with your mother to ask you to help her get back home. I am sorry for the mistakes of my uncle and I will do anything I can to make things right."

"I appreciate that," she told him.

"That's not all," he continued. "I also came here to ask you to stay in Mura with me."

"Stay here?" The idea seemed to surprise her but please her at the same time.

"Merrow, will you marry me and be my wife?"

"Oh, Sebastian!" she cried. Her smile was wide but then it slowly disappeared. "I wish I had known all this before. Mayhap it would have made a difference. But I feel my father's wrath and I am afraid there is no stopping him now."

"Say something to him about us. Explain to him that we want to stay together," said Sebastian, hoping that Merrow really wanted to stay.

"He's read my sister's mind and already knows what happened with my mother. He will never let one of his daughters stay and marry a human from Mura after that."

"Then let me talk to him, Merrow." Sebastian knew this might be his only chance. "I'll get him to change his mind. I'll calm him down."

"Sebastian, there is no changing Father's mind once

it's made up. I'm sorry, but you are only fooling yourself if you think you can stop him."

"Then I'll fight him if need be."

"No, you don't understand. There is no way to stop him or to fight him and win."

"Why would you even say such a thing? Don't you have faith in me, Merrow?"

"Of course, I do, Sebastian." She released a heavy breath. But you are only human. You have no power to go up against my father in a fight."

"So he's a sea monster. I'm not going to let that fact stop me."

"He is more than just that," she told him. "Sebastian, my father is a god of the sea."

* * *

Sebastian felt the heat lodge in his throat and almost choke him when Merrow told him her father was a god. Leading an army of men was one thing. Fighting those with magic was a little more challenging. But to go up against a god was nothing more than a suicide mission. How was he going to remedy this extremely messed-up situation?

"Sea god? Merrow, why didn't you tell me this about your father sooner?"

"I didn't see the need," she answered, looking up at him from the water with those big, round eyes.

"What do you expect me to do?"

"Pull back. I expect you to return to your castle with your men and not even try to fight him. I will try my best to reason with my father."

"Nay. I won't run from a fight, even if he is a god."

"Why not?" asked Merrow. "Because you are afraid your advisor and your men will think of you as weak?

You shouldn't care what they believe, especially since it isn't true."

"I'm a king, Merrow. I lead my men into battle all the time. I will fight to the end, and you will never change my mind."

"Then you'll die by the hand of my father."

"Then so be it. At least I'll die doing what I was meant to do."

There was a loud noise and the waters parted even more as the sea god moved closer to the shore.

"Where is the man who stole and defiled my wife?" boomed Nereus' voice, so loud and powerful that it shook the land. "I also want to see the man who kept my daughter, Merrow captive. I will kill him."

"Nay, Father, stop it," cried Merrow, but the sea god was too angry to heed her words.

"My king. Shall I command the army to attack this monster?" Farrimond was behind him, ready for a war.

"Yes, attack him, my king," ordered Drell. "Do not hesitate. We need to fight him right now."

"Nay. No one uses a weapon unless it is on my order." Sebastian took a deep breath and stepped forward. "Nereus, God of the Sea, I am King Sebastian Ravenwolf of Macada Castle. I am the man who held your daughter. We need to talk."

"You will die for what you did!" Nereus shot a bolt of lightning from his hand. Sebastian raised his sword and prepared himself for the pain he was sure would follow.

"Nay!" Darium Blackseed ran to him, holding out his hands and using his fae power to control the weather. A strong wind blew the fiery bolt to the side, hitting a tree instead of Sebastian.

"Thanks," said Sebastian, looking over to see not only Darium, but also his brothers, their wives, and the

Blackseed boys' mother with them as well. "I didn't expect that from my enemy."

"We're not enemies," said Zann. "We've been trying to help the sea nymphs and have no desire for a battle."

"What's this?" bellowed Nereus. "Some of you have magic?"

"Yes, Father, they do. So leave them alone," said Merrow.

"I will just have to call upon more of my powers then." Nereus threw another firebolt directly at Sebastian. This time, Sebastian deflected the flame with his sword, diving to the ground and rolling, putting out a stray flame that caught his clothes on fire. He was near the shore now and Merrow pulled herself over to him. She was in her sea nymph form and couldn't walk on land, still being a creature of the water.

"Sebastian, are you hurt?" she asked, reaching out to touch his arm.

"Nay," he answered. "Merrow, take your mother and sisters and go through the portal. That is the only thing that might keep your father from killing everyone. No one deserves to die over this."

"I won't leave you," she told him.

"You must," he explained, getting to his feet. "It is the only way."

As Nereus fought against the Blackseed brothers, their mother who was an Elemental of the Air used her powers as well. So did the witch, Medea. Sparks shot everywhere. The sky darkened and black clouds loomed overhead. Wind whipped around them and Nereus started sending high waves to the shore, causing Sebastian's army to retreat. Some of his soldiers were pulled into the water and fought for their lives.

"I don't agree with that plan, Sebastian," Merrow continued to fight him with her stubborn actions.

"Merrow, he might be right." Dee ran to her and hunkered down next to Merrow. "Nereus has a mean temper. He won't stop until he gets what he wants. Mayhap if his family is returned to him, he'll back off and leave Mura forever. We need to try. It is our only chance."

"I'm not sure," said Merrow. "Besides, you are human now, Mother. You will drown trying to go through an underwater portal."

"Not if you and your sisters give her the breath of life while she swims," said Sebastian. "The way you did to me, Merrow. You remember."

"Yes. He's right. It will work. I'm sure of it." Dee stood up and put her hands over her head, waving at them, trying to attract the attention of her husband. "Nereus, it is me. Your wife. Please, stop torturing these poor people. They had nothing to do with what happened to me. That man is already dead."

"What?" Nereus stopped throwing fire bolts long enough to listen. "Doris, I want you to come home."

"I want that too, husband. But how can you still desire me when I have been forced to marry and couple with a human, therefore turning human myself?"

"I don't care if you are no longer a sea nymph. We can be together on land. You know that. Now get home! You have fifty children to tend to."

"Come, Mother. Melite, Galene and Nerites will help you through the portal and give you breath underwater so you won't drown." Merrow held out her hand to assist her mother into the water.

Merrow's siblings popped their heads up from under the water.

"It will be odd to leave here after so long." Dee looked back at Sebastian.

"You need to go. To be with your family," he told

her. "Dee, I can never apologize enough for what my uncle did to you. I am so sorry. If I could change the past, you know I would."

"King Sethor is dead now, so it no longer matters," said Dee.

"I say it does. You will pay for the dead man's mistake, King Ravenwolf." Nereus shapeshifted into a huge bird with sharp talons, a curved beak and scales on his wings instead of feathers. His eyes flashed red with anger.

"Nay, Father. Leave Sebastian alone!" shouted Merrow.

"Go, Merrow! Now. And don't look back." Sebastian lifted his sword, ready to fight, knowing this wouldn't end until he died. That is what the sea god wanted and all Sebastian could do now was to give him his fight while Merrow and her family got through the portal that would take them home.

"Merrow, hurry," called out her brother. "The portal is already starting to close. We need to get through it before it's too late."

"Come, Mother. We will help you." Galene swam to the shore, reaching out to take her mother's hand. Dee took a step into the water, but stopped and looked back at Sebastian.

"I know you and Merrow are meant to be together," she told him. "You are a good man and will make a wise, fair and just king. I have no doubt you would have protected her as well as made her very happy should she have stayed. I am so sorry things have to end this way."

"I want more than anything to make your daughter my wife," he admitted. "Mayhap if I tell Nereus that, he will change his attitude toward me."

"Nay, don't do that. It might make him even angrier. It's too late." Dee shook her head as she sank down into the water. "My husband will not pull back. Once he starts shapeshifting, it means his anger is out of control. He won't stop until he feels his wrath has been carried out. I am so, so sorry." With that, Dee took a deep breath and dove under the water. Merrow's sisters and brother went with her. Still, Merrow stayed, staring at him from the water with tears in her eyes.

"Did you really mean that? That you want to marry me?" she asked him.

"Yes, I do," said Sebastian, swiping at Nereus as the big bird shrieked and dived down, trying to catch him in his sharp talons. Sebastian hit the ground, rolling, stopping at the edge of the water.

"Sebastian!" Merrow swam over, worried for his safety. The bird swept back up into the sky while Sebastian's army drew their weapons. The Blackseeds continued to use their powers against Nereus but they were no match for a god of the sea. Nereus made a huge wave hit against them, landing them all in the water, pulling them out to sea as they tried their best to swim back to shore.

"Goodbye, Merrow." Sebastian reached out and cradled her chin, kissing her sweet lips for the last time. "Never forget me."

"I won't leave you."

"You have to. I don't want you to see me die."

"I need to stop my father."

"You'll only make him more furious. Now quickly, go. Swim back through the portal. It is the only thing that might make your father stop attacking us." He took her hand and kissed it, getting to his feet. Slowly, he let her hand slip from his.

"My king! Behind you," shouted Drell.

Sebastian turned to see that Nereus had

shapeshifted into a dragon now, flying through the sky breathing fire.

"Can this get any worse?" mumbled Sebastian. "Retreat!" he called to his men. "Save yourselves. Go back to the castle." Sebastian would fight to the end, but there was no need for his men to die as well. Nereus wanted Sebastian to pay for his uncle's horrible acts and there was no way out of this now.

"Nay, you must tell them to fight," yelled Drell from atop his horse, doing nothing to assist any of them. "Kill the creature. Kill the Blackseeds. Take the kingdoms of Mura for yourself. That is what your uncle would do."

"Nay," spat Sebastian through gritted teeth. "I will no longer listen to bad advice."

"I am your advisor. You must listen to me, my king. I know what is best."

"We see what your advice has done. I will not let my men or any of the Blackseeds die because of the past stupid choices of my late uncle."

Drell was about to protest again when the dragon's talons knocked him from the horse. Then the dragon breathed fire, killing Drell, burning his body instantly.The dragon flew back up into the sky while Sebastian ran over to find only charred remains of his advisor.

"My king, is he—" Farrimond ran up and stopped abruptly, staring down at the burnt mess.

"He's dead, Farrimond. As will be the rest of us soon. I command you to guide the army back to Macada Castle now! Close the gate and take your posts inside the fortified walls. Protect my kingdom and everyone in it."

"I will, my king." Farrimond bowed. "But what about you?"

Sebastian looked back up to the sky. The dragon was

still breathing fire, about to attack the Blackseeds, who were now emerging from the water after having been swept to sea by Nereus' wave.

"It is me who Nereus wants. I will stay and fight, but first I must see to the safety of the Blackseeds."

"You're going to stay and risk your life for the lives of our enemies?" asked Farrimond. "I don't understand."

"No matter what happens to me, I want you to promise me that you will make sure everyone at Macada Castle knows that the Blackseeds are no longer our enemies."

"They're not?" asked Farrimond.

"They are here risking their lives to help us. They are allies now. Make sure no one ever forgets that from this day on. Now leave! Here comes the dragon again."

"I will do as you command, my king. But let me stay to protect you. Or at least let me send over your squire to help fight for your life."

"Nay. Take Hitch with you and don't let anyone turn back. This is my fight. Even if it ends my life, which it probably will. Now go!"

Farrimond ran off, doing as ordered.

Sebastian heard shouts from the Blackseeds, seeing that the dragon was about to burn them all to a crisp the way it did to Drell.

"Nay! Leave them alone. It is me you want," shouted Sebastian, running down the shore to save his new friends. "Come get me, you bastard!" Still holding his sword, Sebastian reached his arms up into the air, sacrificing himself for the good of so many others.

The distraction worked. The dragon flew toward him, forgetting about the Blackseeds. It swooped down from the sky directly overhead. Sebastian prepared himself for the burning fire that would end his life. Instead, he felt the sharp claws of the beast digging into his flesh as it grabbed him and lifted him up into the sky and then flew out to sea.

"Aaaaaah!" he cried from the intense seering pain. He swiped at the dragon with his blade, managing to slice the dragon's stomach. The dragon shrieked and pulled back, causing Sebastian to drop his sword. It fell into the sea with a splash and disappeared.

"I did nothing to hurt your family," he yelled to the dragon. "That was my uncle who did horrible things but he is dead now, so has paid for his mistakes. All I wanted was to marry your daughter, Merrow. I love her and want to live out the rest of my life by her side."

With Sebastian still in his clutch, Nereus in his dragon's form shapeshifted, turning back into a sea nymph. They hit the water hard, going deep below the surface. Nereus still held on to him, pulling him deeper and deeper under the waves. Sebastian held his breath but realized he would run out of air soon.

Then the sea god released him, and a booming vibration traveled through the water. Nereus in his sea god form shot back up to the surface, leaving Sebastian alone beneath the dark, deep surface.

He was running out of air quickly and had never been this far down in the water before. It was much too far to swim to try to make it to the surface. He would never make it there before he drowned.

That's when he saw colorful ripples of water swirling in a circle up ahead. There was an opening. The portal! He could see Melite and Galene giving their mother the breath of life, pulling her along with them. Their brother, Nerites stood at the side of the portal. It seemed to be closing quickly. Then he noticed Merrow, swimming along behind them.

*I love you, Merrow*, he thought in his mind, hoping she would hear it since it was the last thing he'd ever convey to her before his body perished in the sea.

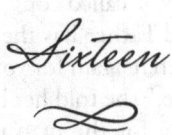

## Sixteen

**M**errow swam underwater along with her family toward the portal, hoping this plan would end her father's wrath and also save Sebastian and all the others' lives in Mura. Sebastian's last kiss had seemed so final. It was hard to believe that she'd never see him, kiss him, or make love with him again. She'd truly lost her heart to him and knew it now since she felt it breaking. Although she didn't want to leave him at a time like this, it was what he'd told her to do. He was right, she supposed. It was their only chance to end this. Once they were through the portal, mayhap her father would leave those on Mura alone, and go home with them, closing the portal behind them forever.

She was about to swim through when she distinctively heard Sebastian's voice in her mind. Odd, since he was on shore and she was so deep underwater in the sea. *I love you, Merrow,* she heard loud and clear. It was enough to make her stop and turn around.

*Sebastian?* She saw what she thought was a figure off in the distance.

*Goodbye, Merrow,* she heard his words in her mind again and knew it was Sebastian this far under the water.

She gasped. He wouldn't survive. Not being this deep. It would only be a matter of minutes before he drowned.

"Merrow, hurry," called out her brother. "The portal is closing and Father has the Calling Conch so I won't be able to open it again for you if it closes."

"Go without me," she told her brother, taking off at a fast swim, heading for the man trapped underwater. Sure enough, she approached and realized that it was Sebastian. His eyes were closed and she was sure he was slipping from consciousness. She needed to act quickly.

Pressing her mouth up against his she blew the breath of life into him, making his eyes open once again.

*Merrow? Am I dead?* he asked, using nonverbal communication.

*Nay, but we must get you to the surface.* Merrow put her arm around his waist, using her strong tail to propel them upward through the deep water. She stopped several times to give him more air. It worked! Before long, they broke the surface. Sebastian coughed and choked and fought to breathe on his own. She had thought they were safe and that the fighting was over. That is, until she heard her father's voice and looked up to see him furious, back in his sea god form.

"Merrow, why did you save him?" bellowed her father. "I thought I killed him. Now, I'll have to do so again."

"Nay, don't touch him!" She put her body in front of Sebastian's, blocking him from her father.

"Move, daughter, before you are hurt."

"I will not move aside just so you can kill the man I love."

"Stop saying such ridiculous things. That man is an evil human." Her father raised his trident in the air.

"Take a deep breath," Merrow told Sebastian, diving

down into the water and pulling him along with her. Thankfully, they'd moved fast enough. The blast of water passed by them but did not touch them. She brought Sebastian to the surface once again.

"Stop, Merrow. I can't keep this up much longer." Sebastian treaded water, struggling to breathe and stay afloat.

"If I stop, my father will kill you," said Merrow.

"I refuse to fight him any longer."

"Wise choice," came Nereus' booming voice. "Now, prepare to die, human."

"I would gladly die for you, Merrow, so don't feel bad when I'm gone." Sebastian put his arm around her and gave her one last kiss. "Remember me always, my sweet, beautiful sea nymph. We will be married, even if it is only in our dreams."

"Stop talking to my daughter that way. You are a human and cannot be trusted. I would never let you marry her. Swim aside, Merrow, and watch your lover die."

"Nay, Father. Please. We want to be married." She spoke the words aloud, but her father didn't want to hear them. Because of what happened to her mother, her father would never trust a human man again. It seemed all he wanted was for all human men to die.

He raised his body up out of the water, only his winding serpent-like tail holding him in this position and still being under the water. Sparks flew from his trident as his eyes turned red. Merrow had never seen her father so angry. This truly frightened her. She had no idea how to help save Sebastian now.

Just as her father was about to strike down Sebastian and kill him, another voice split the air.

"You are not a god of Mura, now leave our people and the land and never return."

"Sebastian? Who is that?" Merrow looked back and forth.

"I'm not sure," he answered. "But it almost sounded like Zoroct."

"Who is Zoroct?"

"The main god of Mura," Sebastian explained. "And look at that!" He pointed up into the sky.

Merrow looked upward to see Elric sitting atop a flying beast that looked to be a wildcat with black stripes and a shaggy mane. The creature had sharp talons and black wings on its back enabling it to fly like a bird.

"It's Elric! What is he riding?" she asked.

"It's called a Stricat. Very dangerous," Sebastian answered. "It appears to help Murians with magic during a battle. I have no idea why it is here to help me."

The Sricat flew with Elric on its back, over Nereus' head. Elric kept materializing rocks, throwing them one after another at her father.

"You heard the god of Mura, now go. Scat. Leave at once," commanded the elf in his nasally little voice. His rocks bounced off Nereus, doing nothing to hurt him. It only made Nereus even more irritated.

"Oh, no!" gasped Merrow. "Elric shouldn't do that. He's going to get himself killed."

"Don't worry. He's too ornery to die," answered Sebastian, actually able to grin now.

"I am Nereus, God of the Sea," shouted her father. "I will not leave until The King of Macada is dead for what he did to my wife, and for also stealing my daughter and holding her as a prisoner."

"That's not what happened, Father. You don't understand," shouted Merrow. "Sebastian is kind. He hasn't hurt anyone."

"Please, explain," came a female voice. When Merrow looked up to the sky again, she saw three apparitions now. They were airy and see-through and looked to be wearing long white gowns. One was a man and the other two were women.

"More gods?" she whispered to Sebastian.

"Yes," he answered "Zoroct is Mura's god of power and might. Hapsren is the goddess of home and hearth, and Cnoir is goddess of love and wealth."

"Sebastian, my father is powerful, but he can't fight off three gods."

"Nay, I don't suppose he can," answered Sebastian. "Hopefully, it will at least cause him to go back through the portal and to leave us all alone."

"Father!" shouted Merrow. "You must leave the people of Mura alone and go back through the portal now. You have mother back, as well as Melite and Galene."

"Someone will pay for the wrong that's been done. I won't leave until that happens."

"We fell through the portal by accident," explained Merrow. "It never would have happened if I hadn't taken Melite and Galene to the Mystic Reef. I'm sorry. So, you see, I am the one to blame and no one else."

"My uncle wronged your wife, and I am sorry for that," said Sebastian. "But I assure you, I would never harm Merrow. I love her."

"You are a human," Nereus growled. "Merrow is a sea nymph. She lives in the sea."

"Not for long," said Merrow. "Father, I am going to marry Sebastian because I love him as well. He is a good man and he makes me happy."

"Merrow, I want to marry you but I don't want you to have to give up being a sea nymph," Sebastian told her. "Your father is right. You do belong in the water."

"Nay, he's wrong," said Merrow. "I belong at your

side. I am more than willing to give up my tail to be your wife."

"You'd be landbound if you did that," her father reminded her. "Besides, you are in a foreign land. You should come home with me. Let's go through the portal, daughter. I will blow the Calling Conch and it will open the portal. Your mother, siblings, and your homeland await you. You don't belong in this place called Mura. You belong in the Aegean Sea."

"It's your choice, sweetheart," Sebastian whispered, still treading water. "I will understand if you don't want to stay. If you want to go home to your siblings and your parents, it's all right, even though I will miss you every day of the rest of my life."

"Father? Can that Calling Conch open the portal to Mura from the other side, any time you want?" she asked him.

"Yes," he answered. "Why?"

"Then I will stay and marry Sebastian. I will give up my tail but gain a soul."

"What about your family?" Sebastian asked her.

"We will start a new family here. Me and you together," she said, holding her arm around his waist, using her tail to keep them afloat. "When I want to see my parents or my siblings, I will reach them with my mind and call to them. Father can open the portal from the other side, and Melite and Galene and the others can come visit us in Mura. Whenever they want."

"Nay, they can't," shouted Elric from the sky. "Our gods won't allow it."

"Elric, hush," scolded the god Zoroct.

"Nereus," said Cnoir. "We will allow you and your family to visit but only if you promise not to cause trouble."

"And to leave when asked," added Hapsren.

"This is not your realm," Zoroct reminded him. "We would expect no different treatment if we were to visit you on your side of the portal."

"So, Nereus, what will it be?" asked Cnoir.

"Don't let any of them stay. They're all trouble." Elric zipped past still sitting atop the Stricat. He manifested another stone and was about to throw it at Nereus when Zoroct stopped him.

"Elric, go home to your little house atop the pinnacle mountain. You are bothering me." Zoroct waved his hand and Elric and the stricat disappeared.

"What happened to him?" Merrow asked Sebastian. "Did he kill him?"

"Nay," answered Sebastian with a chuckle. "You see, Elric is messenger of the gods. But even the gods can't stomach the irritating little man for long. Zoroct just sent him home to the other side of the mountain. The side where the fae and the elves and other magical beings live."

"Oh, I'd like to visit there sometime."

"We can go there whenever you like." Sebastian looked back up at Nereus. "That is, if your father gives us his permission and his blessing to be married."

"I don't need his permission or his blessing," spat Merrow, still very upset with her father.

"Well, I do," said Sebastian, taking her hand in his. "Merrow, I don't want to get married unless your father accepts the idea. I want us all to be happy. I don't need to be always looking over my shoulder, wondering if your father is coming back to kill me."

"Father? Do you agree to our marriage?" asked Merrow.

"I don't like the idea of you being married to a human."

"But you're married to a human now. Mother can never again be a sea nymph," Merrow pointed out.

"That's right," agreed Sebastian. "Please, Old God of the Sea, accept us."

"It's Old Man of the Sea," Merrow whispered.

"What is your answer, Nereus?" asked Zoroct. The gods of Mura still hovered above in the clouds.

"Well...since I cannot fight off three gods, and it seems to be what my daughter really wants, I guess I have to agree to it. But remember, Merrow, this decision cannot be reversed. Ever."

"I know, Father." Merrow wiped a tear from her eye with the back of her hand. "I will miss my siblings as well as you and Mother. But I love Sebastian and really want to be his wife."

"Then so be it." Nereus reached down and patted Merrow on the head. "Goodbye, daughter. Call me if you need me. Or if you long to visit."

"Will my ability to speak to my family in my mind go away once I am human?" Merrow asked her father.

"Nay," he answered. "You will always be a sea nymph deep inside, so that power will stay with you as long as you are not sad, depressed or forlorn."

"Is that why we couldn't hear Mother calling us?" asked Merrow.

"It is," answered Nereus.

"Don't worry, I am sure I will always be happy here," she told the sea god. "I have met so many nice people, and some of them have magic. I cannot wait to find out more."

"It's time to go through the portal," Zoroct reminded him.

"I'm going." Nereus raised the Calling Conch to his mouth and blew. A resounding note filled the air stirring up the water until it started to swirl. This time, the portal was above the water instead of below it. Everyone could see it well. When it opened, Merrow spotted her Mother, her brother and all of her forty-nine sisters peeking through.

"Goodbye, Melite. Goodbye, Galene," Merrow cried out, waving her hand above her head. "Tell Father when you want to come and visit me."

"Merrow, you're not coming home?" Melite looked so sad.

"This is my home now," she replied. "I belong on Mura. With Sebastian." She looked at her husband-to-be and smiled.

"You will make a lovely wife," called out Galene. "Good luck to you both."

"You will be fine, Merrow," called out her mother. "As long as you are with the one you love."

Nereus entered the portal, putting his arm around his wife and looking back. Then, he nodded, and the portal snapped closed. Merrow's family disappeared from sight. When she looked up to the sky, the gods of Mura had left as well.

"We did it, Merrow. I'm still alive and now we can be married." Sebastian let out a happy whooping noise. "Let's get back to shore. I need to thank the Blackseeds for helping us. And I want to invite everyone in Mura to our wedding."

Merrow took her last swim as a sea nymph, heading back to shore. She flopped onto land, running her hand over her tail, her heart breaking to know she would never be able to swim to the coral reef or look for shells with her sisters anymore. Still, she was excited to be able to marry Sebastian and be his wife. She'd be able to visit with her family any time she wanted. Her legs appeared and she stood up. Sebastian took off his tunic and pulled it over her head to hide her naked body.

"Merrow? Are you all right?" he asked. "You seem so sad."

"I'm not sad. Not really. I just guess that I wish there was a way to marry you and stay a sea nymph at the same time."

The Blackseeds were waiting for them on the beach. Sebastian wrapped his arm around Merrow and they headed over to greet their new friends. Once more, Merrow glanced over her shoulder, thinking she was going to see Melite or Galene popping up out of the water, but they weren't there. She was with Sebastian now and would create a new life, living as his wife. As a human. She'd made a good decision, she told herself. It was the right thing to do.

Her eyes scanned the calm sea and she let out a deep sigh. So, if she did the right thing, then why didn't she feel as happy as she thought she would right now? And where was she going to find fifty new friends to replace her siblings?

## Seventeen

"S o the alliance between our kingdoms is secure, Ravenwolf?" Zann asked as he and his brothers and their wives gathered in the courtyard of Evandorm. King Sebastian Ravenwolf, his captain of the guard, and Merrow had joined them as requested.

"Zann, this alliance needs to be with the Queendom of Glint, and with the Fae folk as well," his wife, Lira, reminded him. "We need to wait for your mother and my aunt to arrive."

"They're here," announced Talia, Darium's fae wife. She pointed upward.

Merrow looked up in surprise, to see three women, a man and a dog descending from the sky. They all gently set down right in front of them.

"Are they gods and goddesses too?" Merrow whispered to Sebastian.

"Nay," he told her. "Not at all."

"Then how can they fly?"

"Merrow," said Medea, Rhys' wife, stepping forward. "We'd like you to meet some very special people of Mura. This is the fae queen, Alaina," she said, motioning to the eldest woman of the party.

"Hello, Merrow. I am the mother of Zann, Rhys and Darium," Alaina told her.

"Hello," she answered. "I saw you at the sea, helping to battle my father. Thank you for your assistance."

Alaina nodded.

"This is my aunt, Sasha," said Lira, taking over with the introductions, presenting the second oldest of the females. "She is Queen of Glint."

"Glint?" asked Merrow in confusion.

"It's on the other side of the mountain. The magical side," Sebastian told her.

"Glint is the elven queendom," Lira explained.

"Queendom," repeated Merrow, smiling widely. "I like that. So would all my sisters, I'm sure."

"Do you have a lot of sisters?" asked Sasha.

"Don't ask," Sebastian mumbled under his breath.

"I am Persimmon and this is my husband, Stone," said the last woman.

"Are you an elf or a fae?" asked Merrow curiously.

"Half-elf, half-witch," Persimmon explained. "Elric, the sage, is my father."

"Oh, yes. I know who he is," she said with a nod.

The dog barked, making Merrow jump back. She wasn't used to land-dwelling animals.

"That's just Fang. He won't hurt you," said Stone with a chuckle, hunkering down to hold the dog. "We've already met two of your sisters on the ship. When you first arrived."

"You mean, when we were captured," Merrow corrected him.

Everyone became silent. Finally, Sebastian was the one to speak.

"Honey, no one captured you or your sisters on purpose. It was a surprise to us as well as you to find anything but fish in our nets."

Merrow could have pointed out that she had indeed

been a prisoner of Sebastian, but it no longer mattered. He had changed and he cared for her now. The rest was all in the past. They knew each other better now and were about to get married. "Of course. I'm sorry. I am just a little nervous being here alone."

"You're not alone, sweetheart." Sebastian took her hand in his and gave it a reassuring squeeze. "You've got me. And now, a lot of new friends, as well."

Zann cleared his throat. "So, can we continue with finalizing the alliance?"

"Of course," Sebastian answered.

"Elric, bring the agreement, please," Zann called out.

The elf appeared in a blur, almost making Merrow dizzy. He held a rolled-up parchment in one hand, and a feathered quill in the other.

"I'm still not sure about this alliance," complained Elric. "That is why I have written up the agreement in detail." He snapped his wrist and the parchment un-rolled, hitting the ground since it was so long.

"What's all this?" Sebastian eyed the contract.

"It's nothing to worry about," Darium told him. "It basically says you will never punish, imprison, or kill anyone who has magic again."

"Of course, not." Sebastian looked over at Merrow. "My bride-to-be comes from a magical family as well. It was my uncle who made up those silly rules against magic to begin with. I never agreed with them."

"Good, good," said Elric with a nod. "Then sign it." He thrust the scroll and the quill at Sebastian.

"My king, mayhap I should read over the contract first." His captain of the guard, Farrimond, came for-ward. "Now that Drell is dead, I'd like to take over as your advisor."

"The only advisor I need is Merrow," Sebastian answered. "Besides, making an alliance is all about trust. There is no need to read it. I'll sign it if the Blackseeds assure me it is fair and for the good of all."

"It is." Rhys nodded. "We've all signed it already."

Sebastian looked at the quill and then over at Elric. "I'm afraid you forgot to give me the ink."

"Don't need any," said the elf with a sniff. "It's done by magic."

"Really." Sebastian put the quill to the parchment, and surprisingly watched as his name appeared on the paper. "Interesting." He went to hand it back, but Elric crossed his arms and shook his head.

"Nay. The girl has to sign it too."

"What?" asked Merrow in surprise. She hadn't been expecting this.

"Sebastian is king, and the two of them are not yet married," Farrimond interjected. "There is no need for the sea nymph to sign."

"It's all right. I'll do it," said Merrow, not wanting to cause trouble. She needed all the kingdoms of Mura to be in alliance because she despised war and fighting of any kind. She signed it and handed the things back to Elric.

"Done," said the elf, quickly sticking the parchment and quill into a bag hanging over his shoulder. "All right, let's go then."

"Go? Where are we going?" asked Merrow.

"The wedding," snapped the elf, producing a book from thin air. He flipped it open. "I'm the sage and officiate at any wedding here on Mura."

"You do?" she asked, starting to feel her heart beating faster. This was really going to happen. She was about to become Sebastian's wife. And in doing so, she would turn human, losing her abilities of being a sea nymph forever.

"We weren't expecting this so soon," said Sebastian. "We haven't even had time to prepare."

"What is there to prepare for? Now, let's go. I have things to do." Elric was a very impatient man.

Persimmon stepped forward with her gazing ball in her hand. "Merrow, you look nervous. If it helps at all, I've seen the future in my gazing ball and the two of you are going to be very happily married."

"You saw that? Really?" Why did Merrow's heart ache? She wished for nothing more right now than to have her mother and sisters with her.

"Well, I suppose now is as good a time as any. What do you say, Merrow?" Sebastian took her hands in his and stared into her eyes. "Are you ready to take your vows? It is time to become my wife and queen of Macada Castle."

A wave of intense emotions rushed through Merrow. She closed her eyes and swayed, holding on tightly to Sebastian's arm.

"What's the matter, sweetheart?" asked Sebastian. "I hope you aren't having second thoughts about marrying me."

"No. Of course, not," she said, feeling an odd sensation in her belly. "I just don't feel very well."

"Then let's get this over with quickly," snapped Elric. "This is taking much too long."

"Father, stop." Lira walked over and put her hand on Merrow's shoulder. "Mayhap Merrow just needs a little more time."

"Time," Merrow repeated, noticing bile at the back of her throat. She looked up at Sebastian, feeling even sicker than before. "I'm sorry, Sebastian."

"For what?" he asked.

She turned and vomited, never feeling more embarrassed in her entire life. Especially since she had just ruined their wedding.

* * *

"What's the matter with her?" Half an hour later, Sebastian paced the floor outside one of the bedchambers of Evandorm. "Is she going to be all right? Why doesn't someone come out and tell us something? What is taking so long?"

The women had taken Merrow into the bedchamber to try to heal her. The men all waited out in the corridor.

"She's among healers. The fae will help her," Darium assured him.

"I get a bad feeling about this." Sebastian couldn't help thinking that somehow by this happening it meant their marriage union was cursed. "Why won't they let me in the room?"

"You'll get used to it," said Zann with a yawn. "These women, if you haven't noticed, are extremely controlling."

The door opened and Talia walked out, keeping her back to the door and closing it so the men couldn't see in.

"Did you heal her, honey?" Darium asked his wife. "Is Merrow all better?"

"No, and yes," said Talia, only managing to confuse them all.

"I want to see her." Sebastian headed for the door, but Persimmon came out next and closed the door, blocking his way. "Move aside. I want to enter the room and see my wife."

"She's not your wife yet," Elric said from the shadows. "Mayhap this is all a warning from the gods that you two shouldn't marry after all."

"Don't say that, Father." Persimmon frowned.

"They're too different," Elric continued, waving his short arms above his head. "We don't have sea nymphs on Mura and neither do we need them. We've got enough creatures and magical beings as it is. This marriage will never work."

"Father, Stone and I are very different as well and our marriage has worked out fine," Persimmon pointed out.

"What's wrong with Merrow?" asked Rhys. "Is she sick?"

"We're not quite sure," Talia answered. "Since she is a nymph, we don't really know what's wrong with her or how to cure her. But we're working on it." Talia flashed a smile. "I'm sure she'll be just fine."

"She's probably dying since she's been out of water too long." Elric was much too blunt with his ill thoughts.

"Stop saying those things," warned Persimmon. "That's not true. I saw Merrow and Sebastian in a vision being married and they were very happy. She is not dying, I assure you."

"Can you use your gazing crystal to find out why she is sick? And how to cure her?" asked Sebastian.

"I suppose I can try. Although, I usually see the future. It doesn't normally tell me what is happening in the moment."

"Give it a try, sweetheart," Stone spoke up from the back of the group, sitting on the floor. Fang lay next to him with his nose between his paws. "Your scrying abilities are getting stronger, so mayhap it will work."

"Yes, that's a good idea," agreed Talia. "We've tried everything else, so we have nothing to lose."

Persimmon pulled her gazing orb out of a pouch attached to her belt. All the men moved in closer to watch.

"I'll need room," said Persimmon. "And you do know that I am the only one who can see visions in the gazing ball, so there is no need to try to sneak a peek."

The men all mumbled, complained, and backed away from her.

"Oh. Hmmm. Interesting." Persimmon's fingers grazed over the ball and she peered into it intently.

"Honey? Do you see something?" Stone got up and moved in closer. Fang followed.

"I think so, but I can't be sure. Oh.That is something I didn't expect." Her brows arched.

"What is?" asked Sebastian. "Please don't tell me she has some sort of disease that can't be cured."

"Nay, that's not the case at all," said Persimmon. Sebastian let out a breath he'd been holding.

"Then what is it?" asked Sebastian anxiously. "Is it something that only happens to sea nymphs? Please tell me it's not a curse from any of the gods."

Persimmon chuckled and slipped the gazing orb back into her pouch. "I assure you, she is not cursed. What has happened to her, happens to everyone, no matter if they are magical or not. Or, not everyone. But it does happen to most women."

"What?" asked Sebastian so nervous that right now that he wanted to shake the answer out of the witch. "Tell me. I need to know. What is ailing her?"

A smile spread across Persimmon's face. "Sebastian, Merrow is feeling ill but it isn't because she is ailing. Unless my visions are wrong, I'd say Merrow is pregnant."

Sebastian almost fell over, having to grab on to the wall so he wouldn't collapse. "Pregnant? Already? That's impossible."

"It seems it is possible. Or at least for sea nymphs," said Persimmon. "Like I told you, we really don't know much about them, but now I guess we do."

"Congratulations," said Darium, slapping Sebastian on the back. "You have a head start on your family, it seems."

"You should have let me marry you two when I wanted to," complained Elric. "Now, it's going to be trouble. Trouble, I tell you, with a capital T."

"Elric, what are you babbling about?" asked Zann. "How is Merrow being pregnant going to cause trouble? After all, they are already planning on getting married."

"That's right," said Stone. "Elric, are you just trying to cause problems again? Because, if so, we don't think it's funny." Fang howled, giving his feedback as well.

"You big oafs, wake up!" snapped Elric, pacing back and forth so quickly that it made Sebastian dizzy. "Since she got pregnant before being married, don't you see the concerns?"

All the men looked at one another and shrugged.

"No, not really," said Zann. "Mayhap you need to tell us."

Elric stopped pacing and sighed. Then he jumped up on a wooden bench in the corridor so everyone could see him. "I swear, being a sage and having a brain goes wasted on the lot of you."

"Father, just tell us what you mean. Please," begged Persimmon. "We can't read your mind."

"She's about to be married and turn human, right?"

"Yes," said Sebastian. "But it is Merrow's choice. No one forced her to do it."

"Mayhap that is so," said Elric. "But it is not the baby's choice."

"Explain," said Rhys.

"Don't you fools see?" Elric was becoming angry.

"She was a sea nymph when Sebastian impregnated her. But she'll be a human when she gives birth."

"Is that a problem?" asked Sebastian, not understanding at all.

"It is, if the baby is a sea nymph," spat Elric. "Giving birth to a sea nymph might kill her. Or even if it doesn't, how is she going to raise a child who is half fish? She loses her tail and sea nymph abilities once she's married to you, unless you've already forgotten."

"Oh, no," said Sebastian, feeling as if their marriage would be doomed after all. "I've got to see her." He pushed past the girls and entered the room, needing to talk to Merrow so they could figure out just what to do. This was all something that Sebastian hadn't expected and neither did he know how to fix it.

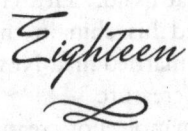

*Eighteen*

"**M**errow? Merrow, honey, it's me. Sebastian." Merrow slowly opened her eyes to discover herself in a bed in the castle with Sebastian standing over her, holding her hands.

"Where am I?"

"You are in Evandorm Castle," he told her in a soft voice. "How do you feel?"

"I'm fine. Why am I in bed?" She sat up, holding her hand to her stomach. "Oh, now I remember. I am sorry for throwing up on the floor."

"No one minds."

"Speak for yourself, you big oaf. Unless you're the one cleaning up the mess, then you'd mind." Elric crawled atop the bed, sitting there staring at her.

"Is something wrong, Elric?" she asked, knowing the little man had something to say.

"You're pregnant, that's what's wrong," spat Elric, making Sebastian cringe. He had wanted to be the one to tell her.

"I am?" Her worried eyes traveled over to Sebastian. "Oh. That's not good, is it?"

"We're not exactly sure," Sebastian answered. "No

191

one here really knows a lot about...about your kind. However, Elric thinks it is unwise to get married now."

"Why?" Her gaze flew over to the elf.

"That's not what I said." Elric crossed his arms over his chest and raised his chin in the air. "I said, you should have gotten married first. Now she'll be a human trying to birth a sea creature."

"Nymph. Say nymph, not creature," Sebastian told the elf under his breath.

"Oh. That is not good." Merrow felt excited at being pregnant but was worried since what the elf said was true. "It could be dangerous, I suppose. If it is a girl."

"What do you mean?" asked Sebastian.

"All girls born to sea nymphs are nymphs," Merrow explained. "But if I have a boy, it could be human since you are human, Sebastian."

"But...if you have a nymph and you are human, how will we raise her?"

"That might be tricky," she said in deep thought. "I don't really know how that would work."

"We need to find someone to ask. Someone who knows all about birthing sea nymphs," suggested Sebastian.

"I know the perfect person to ask. My mother! After all, she birthed fifty-one children."

"And your brother was a nymph too," he pointed out.

"Yes. But my parents were both nymphs. I am sure that is why."

"How can we contact her?" Sebastian let go of her hands and stood up straight.

"The only way to do that would be to go into the sea and call her with my mind." Merrow started to get out of bed, but laid back down when the pain in her belly cramped up once more.

"You're not going anywhere," Sebastian told her, heading for the door. "You stay here. I will do it for you."

"Don't be silly. You can't do that!" Elric was at it again. He didn't seem to be a very positive or supportive man at all.

"I've spoken to Merrow in my mind before. I can do it. Just give me a chance." Sebastian left the room before anyone could stop him.

It wasn't long before Sebastian had boarded The Spectrum with the Blackseed brothers as well as with the ornery little elf. They took the ship far out on the Masked Sea, trying to remember the exact area where the portal had opened before. It would be their best bet to contact Merrow's family on the other side, the closer they could get to the portal.

"Stop here," said Sebastian. "I think this was the area."

Darium and his brothers stopped the boat and dropped anchor.

"Go ahead," said Rhys. "Call Merrow's family with your mind."

"I'll try." Sebastian closed his eyes and thought really hard but nothing happened. "It's not working."

"Perhaps you should get into the water to do it." This suggestion came from Elric. Sebastian didn't really like that idea. Especially since he didn't doubt the elf might convince the others to leave him there and go back to shore without him. After all, up until today they'd all been enemies. He wasn't sure how fast the other kingdoms would really accept him after all the horrible things his uncle did.

"I don't know," he answered.

"If you want to contact sea nymphs you need to do it from the water," said Elric. "It's a conductor of sorts."

"Is that what you all think?" Sebastian asked the Blackseed brothers.

"We have no idea," Darium answered with a shrug. "You are the one who said you've done this before."

"Sea nymphs are a complete mystery to us," added Rhys.

"Well? Are you getting into the water or not?" Zann nodded to the side of the ship.

"I'm not sure." Sebastian looked at the men who were staring at him disappointedly with their arms crossed over their chests. He got the distinct feeling the Blackseed brothers considered this a waste of their time. He shouldn't care what others thought of him, just like Merrow told him. Sadly, he still did. "All right. I'll give it a shot." He stood up, taking off his weapon belt and boots. Then he removed his tunic. "If Elric thinks it'll work, I'll try it. He's a sage and supposedly knows more than the rest of us. I'll go into the water and call for any of Merrow's family with my mind. But if you see a portal opening, be sure to pull me out at once. I don't want to get sucked through it and end up on the other side."

"Got it," said Rhys with a nod.

"It might be better if you did," grumbled the elf. Sebastian thought it best to ignore Elric's comment.

After lowering himself into the water, Sebastian took a deep breath and dove down. He called in his mind for Merrow's family, hoping at least one of them would hear him. *Dee! Melite and Galene. Merrow needs you. Please, hear me. She is ill and I don't know how to help her. You need to come right away.*

He resurfaced several times, but by now the sun was disappearing and it was getting late. He'd had a long day and was tired and drained. All he wanted to do was to go back to his castle and curl up in bed with his arms around Merrow.

"It didn't work," he said, after breaking the surface, feeling more than defeated. Mayhap he didn't do it right. But even if this was so, there was no one who knew anything about this to ask for guidance right now. "No one heard me." He put his hands on the side of the boat and pulled himself up.

"Don't be so sure," said Stone. "It seems your mind is strong enough to call the sirens after all."

"What do you mean?" Sebastian flipped over the side and into the boat.

"Look for yourself." Zann nodded at the sea.

After wiping the water from his eyes, Sebastian looked out at the water. At first he didn't notice anything. Then he saw it. One by one heads popped up in the water until they surrounded the ship completely. They kept coming until there were so many that Sebastian started wondering if all fifty of Merrow's siblings had answered his summons for help.

"Oh, I see," he said, feeling a little intimidated to have so many of them there when his entire army was back at Macada Castle and he had no means to protect himself whatsoever. He hoped Merrow's father wouldn't show up as well. The last thing he wanted after all they'd been through was an attack by undines, especially from the God of the Sea.

* * *

"For the last time, there is nothing wrong with me. Now step aside and let me leave. I need to find Sebastian." Merrow was fully dressed and standing at the open door. Sebastian had requested several of Evandorm's soldiers to guard her door. She'd been told he did it to protect her, but for some reason this didn't feel any different than when he'd held her as a prisoner at his own castle.

"I'm sorry, but we have our orders," answered one of the guards. "We can't let you leave the room."

"Then fetch the lady of the castle. Or one of the Blackseed brothers' wives or mother," she instructed. "I need to talk to someone. Someone with power. Yes, call the women, please."

The guards didn't have a chance to answer before she heard a sloshing sound coming from down the corridor. She peeked out the door to see Sebastian, half undressed and soaking wet. With him, to her pleasant surprise, were her mother and sisters Melite and Galene.

"Mother! Sisters!" Merrow pushed past the guards and ran to them, throwing her arms around the women.

"I'm here too," she heard Sebastian say. She looked over at him, realizing her mistake. He seemed so sad that she hadn't greeted him in the same way as she did the women. Merrow threw her arms around Sebastian and kissed him firmly on the lips.

"Now, that's better." His arms encircled her waist, pulling her closer.

"Why is my family here?" she asked him.

"It's not just us, Merrow," said Melite. "All of your sisters came to your aid when we heard Sebastian's call for help."

"Sebastian summoned you?" She looked from the women over to Sebastian. "You did it with your mind?" she asked him in disbelief.

"Yes," he answered, standing up straighter, seeming so proud. "I did it the way you taught me."

"I see." She almost laughed aloud. Merrow supposed it could be true, but it was highly unlikely. After all, he was only a human. It took someone with magic to be able to call with one's mind and to then be heard through a portal and into a faraway land. Either way, she was touched that he'd do this for her, and loved him for it even more.

"Merrow, are you ill?" asked her mother, putting her arm around her shoulders. "Sebastian said he preferred to let you explain what is going on."

"You didn't tell them?" she asked Sebastian.

"No. Not yet." Sebastian cleared his throat. "I thought mayhap we could do that together. In the privacy of my own castle. Our castle," he quickly corrected himself.

Merrow wasn't sure how she felt about going back to Macada Castle. She liked being around the Blackseed brothers and their wives. Evandorm felt safer. More like home. Everyone here had been so kind to her. They'd also treated her sisters well during their time here. She didn't know anyone at Macada Castle, and wasn't sure those people would be willing to accept her.

"Can't we stay here for the night, Sebastian?" she asked him, hoping he wouldn't object. "I'm not sure how comfortable I feel about going to Macada Castle right now."

"But that's going to be your home now. As soon as we're married," he told her. "Plus, I am the king. I need to get back there anon. My men will wonder what's happened to me. I have obligations that cannot be ignored."

She let out a deep sigh. "I suppose you're right."

"You aren't worried about what my people will

think of you? Or about us getting married, are you?" he asked her.

"Mayhap, a little," she admitted.

"Merrow, you were the one who taught me not to care about such things."

"Yes. You're right." She bit her lip and looked to the ground. He must have known how uncomfortable she felt, because he said something next to make her feel at ease.

"I have a lot to tend to and won't be able to spend time with you tonight anyway. Mayhap, if King Zann doesn't mind, you and your mother and sisters can spend the night here at Evandorm. Without me. I'll be back first thing in the morning."

"You are all welcome to stay." Lira walked down the corridor with Zann. "For as long as you'd like."

"Yes. That's fine," agreed Zann.

"Thank you," said Merrow, feeling a little bad for not wanting to go back with Sebastian, but she really needed to talk to her mother and sisters. Alone.

As soon as the four of them were settled into a bed-chamber and alone, Merrow told them to sit down because she needed someone to talk to who was a sea nymph.

"What is it?" asked Galene.

"You look so sad," remarked Melite, as the two girls climbed atop the large bed, getting close to Merrow.

"Yes, daughter, do tell us what is troubling you." Her mother sat down on the bed, too.

"Mother, I'm worried. It seems...I am pregnant with Sebastian's child."

"Oh, my!" gasped Melite.

"Congratulations," said Galene.

Her mother didn't respond.

Merrow continued. "The elf said since I was pregnant before I was married, once I am human, I might die birthing a sea nymph. Is this true?"

"I'm not sure," her mother answered. "I can't say this has ever happened before. Not with a human and a sea nymph, that is."

"Surely, you'll birth a girl and she'll be an undine," said Galene happily.

"I can't wait to be an aunt," added Melite, bouncing up and down on the bed excitedly.

"I could have a boy. And he might be human. Right?" Merrow asked her mother.

"Not all boys born to sea nymphs are human," answered her mother. "You do have one undine brother, remember."

"Yes, but you and Father were both undines at the time. That's different." Merrow got up and paced the floor, wringing her hands together. "I have to admit, I am having doubts about getting married to Sebastian, although I don't want him know. That is why I wanted to talk with you three privately."

"I figured as much. Come sit back down, Merrow." Her mother patted the bed with her hand. Merrow sat down again, even though she would have rather continued to pace. "You haven't known Sebastian long enough to really realize if you love him and want to be his wife. That is understandable."

"Nay, that's not why. I know I love him and that I want to marry him. It's not him, Mother. It's just...I mean..."

"We know what you mean," said Galene, having read her mind. "The bigger part of it is that you don't want to stop being a sea nymph."

"That's right," she admitted. "Is that selfish of me? I just can't help feeling this way. I am not sure I want to be human, after all. I love the sea, and swimming and life under the waves. I crave everything about it. I also love being with all my siblings." She reached out and took her sisters' hands in hers. "I also like having a tail at times and being able to swim really fast and not have to hold my breath under the water. I look forward to teaching my child, if she is an undine, all about life as a sea nymph. I want her to experience all the things that are special to me. But if I am a human, I'll give up all those things. I won't be able to be that big a part of my child's life, and that makes me sad."

"Well, how do you think Sebastian will feel?" asked Melite. "He'll never be able to spend that kind of time with an undine child under the water, either."

"I didn't think of that," Merrow answered. "I suppose he would feel a lot like me right now."

"There is nothing you can do about it, Merrow." Galene looked to her with sadness in her eyes. "You will marry Sebastian and when you do, you will become human."

"It's not that awful, I suppose," her mother tried to console her. "Besides, you will gain a soul."

"I'd give up having a soul all together if I could only marry Sebastian but stay an undine too."

"That's not possible," said Galene.

"It'll never happen, sister." Melite had tears in her eyes. "Don't worry. We will take care of your child for you and raise her as if she were our own."

"Thank you," said Merrow. "But I can't allow you to take my child back through the portal once it's born. Sebastian and I will want to raise our family here. On Mura."

"It seems to me that you have a difficult choice to make, then," said her mother.

"Mayhap I can birth my baby but never get married

at all?" Even when Merrow said the words, they sounded stupid.

"Your father would never condone that," said Dee. "Merrow, you'd better get married before we go back through the portal. I don't want Nereus finding out about all this by reading my mind when we return."

"Was Father the one to open the portal when you returned?" asked Merrow. "If so, he might already know."

"Nay, it was Nerites," said Melite. "He knows how to use the Calling Conch on his own now."

"I still can't believe that Sebastian was able to reach all of you using his just his mind." Merrow felt proud of him that he should even want to try to help her in that manner.

"What did you say?" asked Galene in surprise.

"I'm proud of Sebastian for calling you with his mind," Merrow answered.

Her sisters looked at each other oddly, and Merrow instantly had a queasy feeling in her stomach. "What is it?" she asked. "Tell me."

"Sebastian isn't the one who called us," her mother answered for them.

"He's not?" Merrow didn't understand. "But that is what he told me."

"He's a human, sister," Melite reminded her. "You know as well as us that he doesn't have the power to call us with his mind. Especially from so far away."

"I didn't think so," she answered, suddenly feeling so silly. "But he sounded so certain that he called you. I guess I wanted to believe him and that is why I didn't question it."

"Mayhap he thinks he called to us, but that is not who summoned us," explained her mother.

"Then who did?" asked Merrow.

"It was that odd little man with the pointed ears," said Galene.

"It was Elric. The sage," her mother told her. "He has more than enough magic to accomplish such a feat. That is why so many of your sisters heard him and wanted to come here to help you."

"Mayhap I'll have to thank him personally." Merrow felt bad for Sebastian and didn't want to tell him that the elf had obviously tricked him somehow. Sebastian would be so upset to think others had made a fool out of him.

"If there is a way to marry Sebastian and stay an undine, Elric would be the only one to tell you how to do that," said her mother.

"Do you think he'll know?" Merrow's hopes picked up. Mayhap she could end up having everything she wanted, after all.

"It's worth a shot." Her mother stood up and stretched. "Merrow, you'd better find him and ask him about it first thing in the morning. I get the feeling Sebastian isn't that fond of Elric. If he knew what you were doing, he might try to stop you."

"You're right," said Merrow. "I shall find and ask Elric about it first thing in the morning." Merrow had a newfound confidence, thinking that Elric might have enough magic to help her with her request. Now, the only problem would be trying to convince him to do so.

"Sister, if he can't help you, are you still going to marry Sebastian and become human?" asked Melite.

Merrow wished her sister hadn't asked that question, because she really didn't know how to answer that right now.

## Nineteen

"**M**y king," called out Hitch later that night, running across the great hall. Sebastian sat in front of the fire with Farrimond and Jocet. He'd been anxiously awaiting the return of his squire for the past few hours now.

"Hitch, did you find out anything?" Sebastian sat with his legs draped over the arm of his chair. He still cradled his tankard of ale on his lap.

"I did, and you won't believe what I discovered."

Sebastian slowly put his feet on the floor. "Jocet, tell the servants and others to leave. I only want you, Hitch and Farrimond to be privy to this information."

"Aye, my king." Jocet got up and started instructing everyone to move far away from them while they talked.

Sebastian thought that something was troubling Merrow more than just being pregnant. He felt as if she were changing her mind about marrying him, even though he hoped that was not true. It made him very uncomfortable. Even though he felt deceitful doing it, he had ordered his squire to stay back at Evandorm and try to find out what Merrow and her mother and sisters were talking about. It was the only way to find out what Merrow really thought about him.

"All right, my king. Everyone but us has moved out of hearing range." Jocet came back to join the group.

"My king, what is this all about?" asked Farrimond, settling himself atop a bench.

"That's what we're about to find out. Go ahead, Hitch." Sebastian nodded and took a swallow of ale.

"It seems you were right, my lord." Hitch pressed his hands together, looking down at his feet. For some reason, he couldn't meet Sebastian's gaze. "The sea nymph is having second thoughts about marrying you, my king."

"Really?" asked Sebastian, not wanting this to be true. "Are you certain?"

Hitch continued. "I was able to get the guard outside their chamber door to tell me this information."

"The guard told you that?" asked Farrimond in disbelief. "So Hitch was spying on them and the guard volunteered this information? That doesn't sound believable to me."

"Oh, all right, so it's not exactly true." Hitch threw his hands in the air. "What really happened was that I got the guard drunk, then listened at the keyhole myself, although I am not proud to admit it."

"Hitch, that wasn't wise to get the guard drunk," Sebastian warned him. "If you were caught, you could have been punished. We just made an alliance with them, and it wouldn't look good for me either."

"Well, my lord, you seemed adamant about knowing what was going on and I could think of no other way to find out," said Hitch in his defense. "The only other thing I could have possibly done is to knock on the door and ask them myself. However, I didn't think they'd really tell me. Plus, it would only look to Merrow as if you didn't trust her."

"You're right, you're right." Sebastian put his feet on the floor and downed the rest of his ale. Then he thunked the tankard atop the table and stood up. "Did she...say anything else?" He was hoping to hear how Merrow felt about carrying his child, but didn't want to come right out and say it.

"Let me think." Hitch rubbed his chin. "I'm parched, my lord and it is hard to talk when I am too dry to swallow." The squire's tongue flicked out to wet his lips. Then he opened his mouth wide and wrinkled his nose, looking like a landbound fish gasping for water.

"Jocet, pour Hitch some of my whisky." Sebastian knew it was what his squire really wanted. Hitch liked whisky more than ale. He liked it twice as much as the rest of them put together.

"Are you sure, my king?" Jocet raised a brow. "Last time he ended up so far in his cups that he stripped naked and climbed the flagpole atop the battlement. We had a hard time getting him down."

"Just give it to him." Sebastian waved his hand in the air, needing this information and willing to do anything it took to obtain it.

"All right." Jocet left and came back with a bottle of whisky and a cup.

"Thanks." Hitch grabbed the bottle, pulled the cork out with his teeth and started drinking right from the bottle, not bothering with the cup.

"That's enough," said Sebastian, pulling the bottle away. "If you stall any longer, I'll throw you in the dungeon for the way you're acting. Now speak. And leave nothing out."

"All right, all right." Hitch let out a belch, made a face and wiped his mouth with his sleeve. "I heard

Merrow say she didn't want to give up being a sea nymph."

"Are you sure?" Sebastian's heart stilled.

"Positive."

Sebastian groaned. "It's over. I knew it." He raised the bottle of whisky to his mouth and took a good long draw. Then, with the bottle still in his grip, he sank back down atop his dais chair. "She'll disappear through that damned portal now with her family during the night and I'll never see her again."

"I'm sure she wouldn't do that, my lord," Jocet tried to calm him. "After all, she seems to love you."

"Yes, she does," said Hitch holding up a finger. "That reminds me of something else she said."

"What?" asked Sebastian, slowly raising his head.

"Hold on. I think better when I'm not so thirsty." He reached out and took the bottle from Sebastian, not shy about taking another swig of whisky. His eyes closed partially and he seemed to be getting very relaxed. He lowered his body atop a bench, a silly smile spread across his face.

"Come on, come on. I don't have all night. Tell me," commanded Sebastian.

"Merrow said she wished she could marry you but still stay a sea nymph." Hitch took one more gulp of whisky. "Aaaah," he said smacking his lips together.

"Why? Why would she say such a thing?" Sebastian was up again and pacing the floor, dragging a hand through his long hair.

"I think it is because that way, she can raise her child as a nymph and her sisters won't take the baby away from her." Hitch looked up as if thinking, and then nodded his head forcefully. "Yes, that was it."

"No one is going to take *our* child away from us."

Sebastian had never considered how they would raise a sea nymph as humans. Mayhap it wasn't even allowed, he had no idea. He couldn't know what kind of silly rules the God of the Sea might have concocted. "Damn, I don't want that. There has to be a way to make this work."

"That's exactly what she said. I think. The guard was snoring loudly, so it was a little hard to hear through the door." Hitch raised his finger in the air again, looking as if he were about to pass out. "There was something else too. Something important. I think. I can't quite remember."

Sebastian stopped pacing in front of his squire, bending over to look right into the boy's eyes. "You'd better remember. If you don't, I swear I will shake the information out of you. Upside down."

Hitch swallowed forcefully, pressing his lips to-gether. "Ah, I remember now. Yes. I have it." He raised the bottle again, but Sebastian quickly took it from him.

"Talk," commanded Sebastian. "And you'd better not forget a thing."

"Merrow is going to see the sage in the morning. Before you get there."

"The sage? Elric? The elf?" asked Sebastian, standing up straight, wondering what was going on. The bottle of whisky dangled from his fingers. "Why? What for? What can he possibly do?"

"I don't really know," said Hitch. "But I heard them say he's got magic that's really strong."

"It's not that strong," said Sebastian with a puff of air from his mouth.

"Yes, it is," answered Hitch. "After all, it was strong enough that he was able to call Merrow's entire family here using just his mind."

Sebastian's head jerked around. "No, he didn't. I did that. I was the one to contact them on the other side of the portal."

"Are you sure, my lord?" asked Farrimond. "After all, you are a human. Isn't that a skill that only those with magic can do?"

This got Sebastian thinking. "I admit it didn't work at first, but as soon as Elric suggested I go into the water —damn it!" What he came up with was something that didn't make him happy in the least. "The stupid elf tricked me!"

Hitch reached for the bottle of whisky Sebastian was holding, but in anger Sebastian threw it across the room. The bottle smashed against the wall.

"Naaaaay," groaned Hitch, watching the liquid drip down to the floor. He covered his face with his hands.

"Elric made a fool out of me," spat Sebastian. "I am sure right now everyone back at Evandorm is laughing at me. Dammit, why didn't I realize this before?"

"Laughing," repeated Hitch, sounding semi-drunk. His hands slid from his face. His eyes were closed.

"I'm going to find that damned elf tonight and give him a piece of my mind!" There was no quenching the fires of anger that burned within Sebastian now.

"How are you going to do that, my lord?" asked Jocet.

"Perhaps you should just call to him using your mind," mumbled Farrimond, doing his best to hold back a chuckle. Jocet couldn't help from smiling as well.

"Shut up! I am king and demand respect from both of you." Sebastian was ready to throw both of them in the dungeon right now. Plus, his squire would follow for telling him these things, even though it was crucial that he know.

"Sorry, my lord." Jocet lowered his head.

"We didn't mean anything by it," said Farrimond, holding up his palms. "I was just breaking the tension with a jest, that's all."

"Breaking tension? Breaking tension?" Sebastian repeated, each time getting louder. "Do it again, and it'll be your neck that is breaking instead, and with my hands clasped around it."

"Aye, my lord," said his captain of the guard in not more than a whisper.

"Farrimond, make yourself useful." Sebastian pointed at the door. "Get to the stable and ready my horse."

"Aye, my lord." Farrimond took a few steps and then stopped, looking back over his shoulder. "You aren't really going out to find the elf at this hour, are you, my good king?"

"I sure am. I need to talk to him before Merrow does. And when I find him, I promise you, he is going to pay for making me look like a fool."

\* \* \*

"Keep up, squire," Sebastian called over his shoulder as they rode their horses in the dark over the steep incline of the Picajord Mountains. They'd been traveling all night, trying to make it to Elric's home which was on a pinnacle mountain just outside of Glint Castle.

"This is crazy, my lord." Hitch yawned, nearly falling off his horse, still feeling the effects of drinking too much whisky. "Why didn't you bring Farrimond instead of me with you? You know I'm no good if I don't get my sleep."

"You're no good even with sleep," grumbled Sebastian. "Besides, I don't want Farrimond anywhere near me right now."

"Because he laughed at you?"

Sebastian hadn't thought Hitch even knew about that since he'd seemed to be sleeping at the time it happened. It was exactly the reason, but he didn't want to admit it to the boy.

"You were the one at Evandorm spying, and who also knows the most about what is going on. Therefore, you should be with me," was all he said.

"Well, I don't know where to find the sage." Hitch yawned again.

"You didn't see him at the castle, did you?"

"No."

"Then he must have gone home. So, that is where we will look for him." Sebastian led the way.

"My good king, the last time we crossed the Picajord Mountains and entered into the land of magic, a war broke out, if I must remind you. It might not be a good idea to come here alone, and in the middle of the night. The elves or the fae folk might consider that a direct threat."

"We've made alliances with them all, so don't worry about it. We'll be fine." Sebastian honestly hadn't thought this over much before leaving his castle in a fit of rage. His squire might be right. It was dangerous at any time for humans to show their faces in the land of magic. Still, it was a chance he had to take. If he was going to be in an alliance with the other kings and queens, he couldn't have the damned elf making a fool out of him at every turn. "We're just about there. I can see the pinnacle mountain with Elric's home atop it from here."

"Another mountain," complained Hitch, looking like he was about to fall fast asleep right atop his horse.

Thankfully, they'd managed to avoid any elves and

fae and made it to the foot of the pinnacle mountain just as the sun started to rise.

"All that's left to do is to go up there and knock on his door and confront him." Sebastian looked upward, realizing it was too steep of a climb to bring the horses. "We'll have to go on foot."

"On foot?" gasped Hitch. "All the way up there? I'm not sure I'll make it." The squire dismounted and collapsed atop a rock. His eyes closed but he jerked awake at the sound of Sebastian's voice.

"I can see you are only going to slow me down. Stay here then and guard the horses. Try to keep your eyes open if that's not too much to ask." Sebastian handed him the reins of his horse. "It'll be faster if I go alone."

"Aye, my lord." Hitch yawned again and leaned back, stretching out his legs.

"If Merrow or anyone from Evandorm shows up, keep them from going to the elf's door until I am done with him."

"Done with him," repeated Hitch, nodding off.

Sebastian hurried up the pinnacle mountain, feeling the burning in his legs by the time he made it all the way to the top. Who in their right mind would purposely live all the way up here? The man must be some kind of hermit. Or addled. Probably both.

Out of breath and feeling exhausted, Sebastian took a look at his surroundings. A bridge led over a crag, leading to a small wooden house with a blue roof directly ahead. The house perched like a bird atop the highest peak, watching down over the Queendom of Glint as well as the Whispering Dale, land of the fae. Sebastian started across the bridge, stopping for a moment to take in the beauty all around him.

To his left, far below, he saw the elegance of Castle Glint. It was a tall castle with balconies and turrets and a bright green roof that couldn't be missed. It was constructed in the shape of a cross, reminding Sebastian of a church. Outside the ornate golden gates of Glint lay the village. Each home of the elves was encircled by tall hedges, almost making a privacy barrier, or perhaps a protective natural setting. When he fought the elves in the past, under the command of his uncle, he never realized how beautiful and green their land had been. Now he felt bad for the past lives he'd taken. This elven homeland seemed so peaceful and serene.

He looked to his right and could see down upon the colorful little dainty cottages that made up the Whispering Dale, land of the fae. From his position, he could tell the fae lived in a beautiful paradise of tall colorful flowers and crystal clear lakes. The scent of Lippenbur Lilies drifted all the way up the mountain, smelling sweet and magical, making his senses tingle. He tried not to breathe in the aroma of these flowers, having heard that the lilies contained an aphrodisiac that made anyone and everyone lustful, wanting to mate.

He could see lots of butterflies, dragonflies, and all the brightly colored roofs dotting the landscape. Just beyond the fae village was a lake with the pyramids of the gods. Near the shore were the Quamm Caves inhabited by those pesky gnomes they'd had to fight when King Sethor met his demise. But as dangerous as all these places were, his attention was drawn to the most dangerous of all. Across the water was the Isle of Denwop, inhabited by giants. He shivered, remembering the battle against these beasts that had occurred in the near past. It was something he never wanted to experience again.

Having made his way to Elric's front door, Sebastian raised his fist to knock. He stopped himself when he was sure he heard voices coming from inside. Putting his ear to the door, he listened, the same way Hitch had done in Evandorm when he first found out all this disturbing information. Sebastian heard female voices from within. He recognized Merrow's voice immediately. Frustration swept through him. He had wanted to set the elf straight before she showed up. Now he wouldn't have a chance to do that because he didn't want her watching as he strangled the life out of the irritating little man.

He barged into the room, stopping in his tracks when he saw Merrow, Medea, Lira, and Dee. He knew immediately how they'd gotten here so fast. Medea had used her witchy powers to transport them here. His trek over the mountains and traveling most the night was done in vain. He knew that now. Sometimes it was daunting to be a mere human.

"Sebastian?" Merrow blinked twice. "What are you doing here?"

"Surprised to see me, are you?"

"Yes," she answered. "I didn't expect you to show up here of all places."

"Why not? What are you keeping from me?" he asked, wanting to give her a chance to come clean with him.

"Nothing." She looked down and kicked at the floor.

"Elric, I'll have a word with you." Sebastian tried to control his anger, not wanting to come across as an ogre in front of the women.

"Why is everyone pestering me so damned early in the morning? Why are you even bothering me at all?" complained Elric, his hands waving in the air dramatically as he spoke. "Can't a man have a little privacy? After all, I'm living on the top of a mountain. Why is this place so busy? What is wrong with all of you for even coming here at all?"

"Elric," Sebastian spoke up. "It's been brought to my attention that you've tricked me, and I don't like it in the least." He said it in front of everyone, no longer caring since they obviously already knew.

"Tricked you?" Merrow looked over at the elf. "Elric, what exactly did you do to Sebastian?"

"Nothing." This time, Elric looked down and kicked at the floor.

"Father, tell us the truth," Lira said, giving him a stern look. "You've been up to your old tricks again, haven't you?"

"He made a fool out of me," Sebastian blurted out. "I am a king of Mura and deserve some respect."

"Sebastian, calm down," said Merrow. "I am sure whatever this is all about, it was just a misunderstanding."

Sebastian could no longer hold his tongue. "The stupid sage tricked me to get in the water, knowing damned well I was human and couldn't call to sea nymphs with my mind."

"Oh, that." Merrow flashed him a sympathetic smile.

Sebastian wasn't done yet, and kept on talking. "Then, he called your family himself, Merrow. It wasn't me who contacted them, but you know that already, don't you? Yet, everyone let me believe that I had done a great thing on my own."

"I'm sorry, Sebastian. I didn't know about it until after you left Evandorm," Merrow told him.

"It was amusing and really livened up my day." Elric had the nerve to laugh.

"Nay, it was embarrassing, and I don't like the feeling." Sebastian reached out for him, but Elric was too fast. He sped away. Sebastian knocked over a chair trying to get him, but once again the little man zipped away in a blur and ended up at the opposite side of the room.

"Damn you! Stay still so I can strangle you." Sebastian dove over the table, landing hard, once again missing Elric completely.

"I'm bored with this game." Elric sat in the open window biting at a hang nail. "Are we done yet?"

"Nay, I am far from finished. You will pay for what you did," Sebastian warned him. He was so mad at him that he wanted to push the elf out the window. But before he could even try, Merrow grabbed him by the arm.

"Sebastian, stop it. This isn't like you. No one is laughing at you and never was."

"I was," said Elric, laughing aloud again.

"Please," Merrow said in a half-whisper. "You are better than this, Sebastian. Don't let him upset you. It's not worth it."

Merrow's words brought Sebastian back to his senses. He took a deep breath and released it, trying to regain his composure. Part of him was glad Merrow had stopped him from killing the sage. The elf probably would have moved aside so fast that Sebastian would be the one falling out the window instead.

"I was only trying to help." Elric patted his mouth as he yawned.

"Elric, we are here to ask you for more help," said Dee.

"You are? Why? What about?" asked Sebastian, not knowing exactly what they were up to, and fearing it had something to do with their wedding. He hoped Merrow wasn't going to back out now.

"Yes, Elric, we need your help," agreed Merrow, her gaze drifting over to Sebastian. "Sebastian, I'm sorry that I didn't talk to you about this first, but you should know that I have had second thoughts about getting married."

"I know," he said softly. "I've heard."

"You know? How?"

Now, he'd done it. He'd have to tell her the truth. If he didn't, and she found out he'd sent a spy, she'd be furious that he'd lied. That isn't what he wanted at all. A marriage based on lies was never going to work.

"I have to admit Merrow, I figured you didn't want to marry me and I wondered why. That is why I had Hitch spy on you."

"You did?" all the women said at once.

"Oh, boy. You are in trouble now, you fool." Elric hopped off the table laughing. He zipped over to the stove. "Who wants tea? Mayhap a little pazzleberry pie too? We need some refreshments because this is about to get entertaining."

"Sebastian? You were spying on me?" Merrow looked hurt.

"I'm sorry, sweetheart. I should have just come out and asked you. I guess deep down I was afraid to hear your answer and that is why I was hesitant to even know."

"You were deceitful," said Merrow, her eyes narrowing. She crossed her arms over her chest.

"Merrow, you weren't honest with Sebastian either," her mother pointed out. "If you had been, he would be included in trying to figure out how you can still marry him and stay a sea nymph."

"What? Is that what this is all about?" asked Sebastian.

Merrow let out a long, deep sigh. "Mother is right. I should have come to you with my concerns. Can you ever forgive me for going behind your back?"

"Only if you can forgive me." Sebastian took her hand and kissed it.

"I'm going to retch if you two keep that up. Now do any of you want tea or not?" The elf held a kettle of hot water.

"No, thank you," said each of the women in turn.

"Nay," answered Sebastian, his eyes still fixed on Merrow.

"Fine!" Elric slammed down the tea kettle and his arms were waving above his head again. He was a strange little man who seemed to fly off the handle with tangents for no reason at all. "I get woken up at the crack of dawn and can't even have a cup of tea before I'm being bothered by fools and big oafs. What do you all want from me?"

"Elric, I was hoping you'd know a way for me to marry Sebastian and still stay a sea nymph instead of turning human," Merrow explained.

"Why in the name of Belcoum would you want to do that?" Elric cursed, using the name of Mura's god of the underworld.

"Because I like being an undine." Merrow shrugged. "I also want to be able to raise my child as a sea nymph. Is that so bad?"

"Will you for sure become human as soon as we're married?" asked Sebastian, just to make sure he understood this and how it worked.

"Yes," said Merrow. "I'll give up my tail and my life as a water nymph and be landbound and human forever from then on. There is no reversing my decision."

"You said you'd gain a soul," Sebastian pointed out. "Sweetheart, would it really be so bad to be human and have a soul? Your mother is human now, yet she is still living with all the sea nymphs, although she's on land."

"I'd like to make something clear," Dee spoke up. "I

only tolerated being human because I did not have a choice when I was forced to marry an evil man I hated. However, this time it will be my daughter's choice to become human. It is her life. She is right to question it and think things through before making such an important decision."

"Sea nymph, I don't know how you'd be able to do what you are asking me about," said Elric. "Sorry, I can't help."

"Oh. All right, then." Merrow's sad eyes turned downward. "Thank you, anyway, Elric. I had to ask." She turned and started walking to the door.

"Wait a minute," said Sebastian, not wanting Merrow to have to give up all she loved just for him. "Elric, you said you are a messenger of the gods of Mura."

"Yep. That's right. What of it?" Elric zipped over to the door. "Do you need a message delivered to them? It's not common or usual to have a human request the audience of a god and not advised at all."

"I understand that," answered Sebastian. "But can't you ask your gods if they can use their powers to let Merrow be able to marry me but stay an undine?"

"Can you? Can you do that, Elric?" Merrow looked to the elf with wide eyes.

"Nope. I can't bother them with silly nonsense like that. Sorry. Time for you all to leave now."

"Father!" scolded Lira. "These people came here seeking your help since you are the wise sage of Mura."

"Wise ass is more like it," said Sebastian, covering his words with a fake cough.

"You can't turn these people away," Lira continued. "Besides, you know as well as I that you can so ask the gods. So, ask them to do this small favor."

"So you...lied to us? Really, Elric?" Sebastian raised a brow, not at all surprised to hear this. He said it only to point the finger at someone besides himself or Merrow.

"You don't want to help me." Merrow blinked away a few tears.

"Please, help my daughter, Elric," begged Dee. "I lived for years being so unhappy and will not let that happen to my daughter as well. Merrow doesn't deserve to be sad just because she fell in love with a human."

"Elric?" Medea stared at him.

"Father?" said Lira, glaring at him as well.

The elf crossed his arms over his chest and scrunched up his nose. Then he lowered his head and looked up at them, showing the whites of his eyes. "Fine," he muttered. "I'll do it. However, I can't promise they'll want to help someone from beyond the portal, so don't get your hopes up. The gods are not known to be gracious or even fair."

"Merrow is one of us now, Father," Lira reminded him. "She's going to stay in Mura, so this is not a request for someone beyond the portal. This is her home now. Why wouldn't they want to help her?"

"Especially since Sebastian has made an alliance with the rest of the kingdoms, and queendoms," Medea pointed out.

"I said fine," the elf answered through his clenched teeth. "What else do you want from me? Now everyone, out! Leave me alone. Gooooo!" He ripped open the door. Hitch was right outside with his ear pressed up against the door. He had fallen asleep in a standing position. He immediately began to fall.

"Arrrgh!" yelled Elric, just managing to dash out of the way before Hitch hit the floor with a loud thump. The squire's eyes popped open and he sprang to his feet.

"My king, I heard something you should know about," said Hitch, looking only at Sebastian. "They're going to send Elric to the gods to ask them...something." He scratched his head. "I might have missed part of it since I was soooo tired. Wait a minute. You're here." He seemed to be trying to make sense of everything and where he was.

Everyone laughed, and Hitch spun around in surprise, his hand going to his heart.

"It's all right, squire, I already know all that," said Sebastian. "Now, let's get you back to the castle and off to bed before you fall right off this mountain."

*Twenty*

Sebastian stood looking out to sea over the sidewall of his ship, The Thunderbolt. A fitting name since Nereus could very well show up at any minute and start throwing lightning bolts at him again. It hadn't taken even an hour to get the news back from Elric that the gods and goddesses of Mura would not help Merrow with her request.

Sebastian's new alliance members which included all of the Blackseed brothers, Stone, and all their wives, as well as the fae queen, Alaina, were with him at his request. Merrow and her mother were there too, as well as Elric, Farrimond, Hitch, and Sebastian's crew.

Hitch walked up next to him. "My king," he said, still yawning since he'd never had any real time to sleep yet. "Tell me again. Why are we sailing out to sea? And with so many of our enemies?"

"They're not our enemies anymore and don't forget it," Sebastian warned him. "Everyone aboard this ship is now our ally."

"However, that might change soon." Elric sped over and climbed atop the sidewall to sit down. "As soon as you foolishly try to conjure up the sea god, that is."

"Who? What?" Hitch's head moved back and forth as he looked to Sebastian and then Elric, standing between them both.

"I'll explain." Merrow came over to join them. "The gods of Mura won't help me because they are afraid if they do, my father will be angry and start a war."

"That is why she should just go right back through the portal and take all these blasted sea nymphs with her." Elric glared down into the water and made a face at Merrow's sisters who were swimming alongside them. So many of her sisters were still there, waiting for her to make her decision on whether she was going to stay and marry Sebastian, or come home with them.

"I'm not going anywhere, Elric," said Merrow, slipping her hand into Sebastian's. "I only came to bid farewell to my mother and sisters."

"Then you're really going to marry the oaf?" asked Elric, shaking his head.

"Yes, I'm going to marry Sebastian, and he's not an oaf," she said, smiling up at Sebastian. "I'm already carrying his baby and we will raise our child together." Her hand covered her belly.

"As a human?" asked Hitch.

"Yes, that's right," Merrow answered.

"Nay, that's wrong." Sebastian released her hand and stood up straighter.

"What do you mean?" asked Merrow. "You no longer want to marry me?"

"Of course, I do. But I won't let you give up being an undine just to be my wife. I know how much it means to you."

"We don't have a choice," said Merrow. "Not if we want to be married, and not just live together while raising our child."

"There is one more thing we can try, and I intend to

do so right now." Sebastian looked over to his captain. "Owaine, drop anchor right here."

"You're dropping anchor to let them off the boat, right?" asked Elric.

"Nay. I have another plan, and I only pray that it works."

"What are you going to do, Sebastian?" asked Merrow with concern in her eyes.

"Summon your father, Merrow," he told her, feeling nervous but knowing this was something he needed to do.

"What?" Elric, Hitch and Merrow said at the same time.

"Nay, don't do that, my lord," said Hitch. "It was hard enough trying to get rid of him the last time he was here."

"He has to open the portal anyway. Now call him," Sebastian instructed.

"My brother can open the portal," said Merrow, shaking her head. "I agree with the others that it is a bad idea to summon my father."

"I need him here because I am going to personally ask him to grant your request to marry me but to also stay a sea nymph."

"Really? You'd do that for me?" asked Merrow, a blush staining her cheeks.

"Of course, I would. I love you, sweetheart and I want you to be happy."

"Nay," she said. "I—I don't think my father has the kind of power to grant that request."

"Why not? He's a god of the sea, isn't he?" asked Sebastian. "I thought gods could do anything."

"Yes, but I don't know if this is a good idea," she said.

"Nereus can grant the request, but I can't guarantee

he will." Dee walked up to join them. "Merrow, if Sebastian is willing to risk everything to ask your father for this favor, then you need to let him try."

"Not if it's going to get us all killed," spat Elric. "Oh, you really are stupid, just like the Blackseed boys." Elric zipped away to the other side of the ship.

"That's why you asked so many to join us today, wasn't it?" asked Merrow, figuring out Sebastian's plan. "You knew you were going to do this and wanted the Blackseeds and the other men and the women with magic here to help if my father should object and attack you."

"I was only thinking about the safety of everyone on Mura," Sebastian admitted. "I am a king. I think ahead and take precautions."

"My lord," said Hitch. "Perhaps the best precaution is not to call him at all."

"I agree," shouted Elric, leaning back and closing his eyes.

"Nay, Sebastian's right," said Merrow. "I have to let him try. All right, I will call my father now."

Sebastian watched nervously as Merrow closed her eyes and summoned her father in her mind. He swore he could hear her, but realized it was only his imagination. After all, he didn't have this ability. He was only human.

"Sister, what are you doing?" Galene swam over to the side of the ship. Melite was with her.

"We hear you in our minds calling for Father. Is that a good idea?" asked Melite.

"Sebastian wants to talk to him," explained Merrow. "If we're going to be married, he can't keep ignoring Father. It will be all right."

"If you say so." Melite didn't sound at all like she agreed with this plan.

"Something's happening," said Hitch, his eyes opening wide. "The sky is darkening and the waters are becoming turbulent."

"It's the portal. It's starting to open." Sebastian felt his stomach clench. "Nereus is arriving."

"Take a deep breath and try to stay calm," Merrow told him. "And please be careful how you speak to my father. He tends to take things the wrong way a lot of times."

"I can think of more relaxing things to do, believe me." Frantic thoughts ran through Sebastian's head. Was this a foolish idea after all? Was he endangering them all? Did he have a death wish? He was starting to wonder what he'd been thinking when he came up with this plan. Still, he was determined to do it for Merrow. He would do whatever he could to make this turn out right in the end, and to ensure his bride-to-be remained happy.

The waves of the sea parted, and all the sea nymphs huddled together. First, Merrow's brother came through the underwater portal.

"Father is furious that so many of his children went through the portal," said Nerites as soon as his head popped up from the water. "Everyone needs to get home at once."

"Not yet," Sebastian called out, standing tall and proud on the bow of his ship. "I need to speak to Nereus before anyone leaves."

"Nay. Not you again," groaned Nerites seeing Sebastian. "This won't end well," he warned him as the father of the sea nymphs made his presence known.

First came the prongs of his trident, then his crown upon his head rose from the water. Then the one who was referred to as the Old Man of the Sea lifted up majestically, his serpent-type tail whipping out of the water behind him.

"Why have you summoned me here, Merrow? What is this all about?" bellowed Nereus looking meaner and angrier than last time.

"It was me who summoned you, through Merrow," Sebastian spoke up, not wanting Merrow to get in trouble.

"I have nothing to say to you, human," said Nereus, spitting into the sea.

"Father, his name is Sebastian," Merrow interjected. "Please, listen to what he has to say. It is important."

"Why should I?" The sea god lifted his trident in the air and lightning bolts shot out of the prongs.

"Please, don't do that, Your Majesty," said Sebastian, diving out of the way of a stray bolt. His crew ran to all corners of the ship. "I did not summon you so the gods of Mura could fight you again."

"What other reason would there be?"

"I called upon you, with only Merrow's sake in mind. She wants to marry me but does not want to give up being a sea nymph." Sebastian cringed, waiting for the sea god to explode with anger.

"That's not how it works," shouted Nereus, frowning. "If my daughter marries a human, she becomes one. She can no longer be an undine. She needs to decide, and can't have it both ways.

"But Father, I need to stay a sea nymph. It's important," cried Merrow.

"Then don't marry the human. Simple as that." The wind blew Nereus' long hair up into the air. His beard was down to his waist.

"You don't understand." Merrow looked over to Sebastian with tears in her eyes.

Sebastian took a deep breath and slowly released it.

Merrow was being so brave, standing up to such a stubborn father. Sebastian had lost his parents early in life and never had to confront them in this way. He wasn't going to let her do this on her own. There was only one thing to say that could possibly change Nereus' mind. As reluctant as he was to have to tell him, Sebastian realized he had no choice.

"My king, I've prepared the men to fight," said Farrimond from behind him.

"My brothers and I are ready as well," said Darium who had also joined them. They all had their hands hovering over their weapons, ready to use them at a moment's notice. "The women are also ready to use their magic if needed."

"Nay. There will be no fighting," Sebastian told them. "No one will draw a weapon without my knowledge. Understand?" Sebastian turned back to the sea king. "Your daughter wants to be able to raise our child as a sea nymph and cannot do that if she is human. You see, she is already pregnant by my seed."

Nereus exploded in anger just like Sebastian expected him to do. Waves crashed up against the ship, causing it to roll to one side. The Blackseed brothers and their wives all hung on to whatever they could so as not to be thrown overboard.

"Now you did it, you fool," he heard Elric mutter from somewhere. Sebastian looked up to see the elf pulling himself back over the sidewall. He was sopping wet.

"I love her! I want her to be happy but only you can help. Please," begged Sebastian. "Use your magic to grant her the request. Please, let Merrow be my wife, but still be able to keep being an undine as well."

Sebastian had no chance to hear an answer. Nereus' anger was all directed at him. Sebastian took a blow to the chest from a firebolt from Nereus' trident. It paralyzed him and he couldn't move. His legs went limp, his body bending over the rail of the ship. Then, when the ship rolled back in the opposite direction, Sebastian toppled over the railing, falling into the black depths of the Masked Sea.

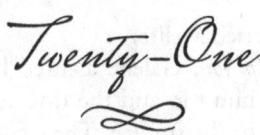

# Twenty-One

"**N**ay!" cried Merrow as she watched Sebastian's body hit the water. "Father, what have you done?" she screamed. "I love Sebastian. I would do anything for him."

"Anything but turn human," her father answered snidely.

"It's all about our child. Your grandchild." She put her hand on her belly. "If you won't help us, then leave Mura at once. I never want to see you again."

With that, she dove into the water, immediately feeling her tail and fins emerge. *Sisters, help me to find Sebastian,* she called out in her mind. *"He is paralyzed from Father's firebolt and cannot swim to save himself. Please, help me find the man I love."*

*He's this way,* Galene called out in her mind. Merrow saw where she pointed and sped in that direction. Since she could swim faster than all her sisters, she made it to Sebastian first. He was doubled over and sinking fast. His eyes were closed and he looked half-dead. She had to act quickly.

The first thing she did was to pull him close to her and give him the breath of life. Then she put her arm around him and tried to swim to the surface, taking him with her. Unfortunately, her father was stirring up such a fuss that the ocean current was strong. Too strong for one sea nymph to successfully save a human in such turbulent waters.

*We're here,* cried Melite.

*We will help you,* Galene assured her. Galene and Melite grabbed him too and the three of them tried to bring Sebastian to the surface. Their father was still too angry, and didn't allow that to happen. Once again, Merrow gave Sebastian breath, but she was tiring quickly from fighting her father's wrath as well as struggling against the sea.

*Father is too strong. Too angry,"* she told her sisters in her mind. *He will not let me surface with Sebastian.*

*We're trying, but are not strong enough to help you,* came Melite's thought.

*Three sea nymphs are no match against the God of the Sea,* was Galene's reply, and Merrow knew she was right.

*Mayhap three can't do it, but what about fifty?* asked Merrow.

Merrow looked around to see all her sisters and even her brother swimming as fast as they could toward them. Her heart almost exploded with happiness and love. All of the sea nymphs worked together, managing to fight against the forces of nature as well as their father to bring Sebastian out of the water. As soon as his head broke the surface, the siblings all cheered aloud.

"Father, that wasn't nice," Merrow scolded him. "Now, release your magic on Sebastian and let him go free. He only summoned you because he knew how much it meant to me. I want to be able to raise our sea nymph child, if that is what she is, in a way that you would be proud of."

"What's this?" asked Nereus, realizing all his children had worked against him to help save Sebastian.

"Nereus, our children have accepted Sebastian and so have I," Dee told her husband. "If you don't grant Merrow her request, I am not coming back home."

"Neither will we go back through the portal," called out Galene.

One by one all of the female sea nymphs agreed.

"Nerites, get your sisters back through the portal now," commanded Nereus.

Her brother hesitated, then answered. "Nay, Father, I won't," boldly said the sea nymphs' only brother. "I have to admit, I agree with Mother and my sisters. Merrow loves Sebastian, even if he is human. And I, for one, would like to be able to see my niece or nephew growing up. Hopefully as a sea nymph. But that is up to you now."

"Arrrrrrgh," shouted Nereus, rumbling the air with his powerful voice. "I can't do that. If so, others will view me as weak."

Sebastian stirred in Merrow's arms, opening his eyes and actually able to speak.

"You are not a weak king," he told Nereus. "You are the strongest king I've ever met. Why would you worry what others might think of you? A wise woman once told me to do what I feel in my heart is the right thing to do. Not to live in fear of what others will think of me if I go against what is expected of me. Please, King Nereus. Grant us this one request."

"She should never have gotten pregnant at such a young age," snapped Nereus.

"Forgive me, Sire," said Sebastian, still holding on to all the sea nymphs to stay afloat. "But Merrow is one hundred and fifty years old. By Mura's standards, that is already almost three times longer than any of us live in a lifetime. She is not too young, I assure you."

"Nereus, if you'll think back, I was pregnant with

your first child before we got married as well," Dee spoke up. "Grant our daughter her wish. Let them marry, and let's go home."

"If I do this, will the rest of you, besides Merrow, come back through the portal? Will you return home where you belong?" asked Nereus.

"Yes," they all answered one by one. All but Galene and Melite.

"I didn't hear an answer from you two," said their father, knowing exactly who answered and who did not.

"I like it here on Mura, Father," said Melite. "I wouldn't mind staying."

"I feel the same way," agreed Galene.

"It is all of you, or I won't grant the request," came Nereus' final words.

"Merrow, I don't want to leave you." Melite cried and clung to Merrow.

"The three of us are so close," Galene pointed out. "It won't be the same without you."

"If Sebastian agrees, you two can come visit and stay as long as you want whenever you want." Merrow looked out to the rest of her siblings. "That goes for all of you. Mother, too."

"I agree," Sebastian answered, his teeth chattering together, feeling the effects of the cold sea. The nymphs continued to hold him to keep him afloat.

"Nereus? What will it be?" asked Dee. "I, for one, know how lonely it is not to see my family. I have had eight years to experience this emptiness and it is nothing anyone should ever have to go through. I think this is a generous offer to let the nymphs visit Mura whenever they want. We should take it."

"We?" asked Nereus, his male pride showing.

"You," answered Dee with a kind smile.

"All right, then. I grant you your request, Merrow."

Nereus waved his trident in the air, and Merrow felt the energy go right through her. "You can marry the human now. You'll be in human form while on land, but once you feel the water you will be an undine once more. I'll remove the curse on the human as well so he can move on his own."

"Thank you, Father!" exclaimed Merrow. "Thank you for making me so very happy. Now I can be with the man I love."

"Everyone, back through the portal," Nereus commanded.

"Wait!" Sebastian called out, finally able to move his limbs once again. "I would like—we would like you all to stay at least long enough to attend our wedding."

"Yes!" cried Merrow. "I would love that."

"So would we!" Melite spun in circles in the water and Galene dove down and slapped the water with her tail.

"Sebastian, how quickly can we get married?" asked Merrow.

"We have the elven sage on board, as well as all of our new friends," Sebastian answered, giving her a quick kiss on the lips. "That's all we need. If you want, we can get married right now."

"I'd like that. Let's do it," she told him. "I don't want to wait a minute longer."

The sky cleared up and the waves subsided. The sun came out just in time for everyone, gods, nymphs, magical beings and humans, to join together as one. They were all here to participate in the wedding ceremony between a human and a sea nymph, an event that would change things on Mura forever.

## Twenty-Two

"This is ridiculous, you fool. Do this on land," complained Elric, standing at the bow of a row boat with Darium rowing. Merrow's mother sat at the back of the boat. They stopped out in the sea where Sebastian waited with Merrow in her sea nymph form to be married. Her sisters all surrounded her in the water, and even her father and brother watched from a distance. Owaine brought The Thunderbolt out to meet them, with everyone else on board.

"Nay, Elric. This is where we want to be married," Sebastian told him. "Out at sea." He treaded water, looking over at Merrow and giving her a big smile.

"Sebastian, we can go on land to be married," Merrow told him. "This isn't necessary."

"No, we won't. We will stay here. I wouldn't have it any other way." Sebastian took one of her hands in his. "This way, your family can all be a part of the wedding and experience it up close. Elric, hurry up and say our vows. I'm not sure how much longer I can keep treading water."

"Had I known you'd like being in the water so much, I never would have tricked you to go into the sea in the first place," griped Elric.

235

"You can come in and join us, Sage." Sebastian chuckled.

"I think not!" Elric stuck his nose in the air.

"Let me and my sisters help you stay afloat, Sebastian. Melite, Galene," Merrow called out.

"We're here, sister." Galene held on to Sebastian.

"We won't let him drown," said Melite, doing the same. "Go ahead and take your vows now."

Merrow's heart swelled with love. No man she ever knew—no human man—would go to such extremes just to marry her. First, he'd risked everything by approaching her father because he knew she wanted to remain a sea nymph. He'd been so fearless, not caring what his loyal men thought of him. She loved him for that. And to actually marry her right here in the water was the most romantic thing she could imagine.

"All right," grumbled Elric, standing on the bench of the boat, raising his hands in the air. "Since I hate being out here, this is the shortened version. Sebastian Ravenwolf, do you take Merrow as your wife?"

"I do," he said, reaching up and kissing Merrow while her sisters helped him to stay afloat.

"And do you, Merrow Havfine, take Sebastian to be your husband?"

"Yes. I certainly do." Merrow returned the kiss.

"Then you two are hitched. Do whatever you need to do."

"Elric, thank you." Sebastian swam to the rowboat and held out his hand for a shake.

"Whatever." Elric reached down to take his hand. When he did, the rowboat shifted, Elric lost his balance, and he ended up in the water. He surfaced spitting water from his mouth.

"You big oaf, you did that on purpose," screamed Elric.

"Sebastian? Did you?" whispered Merrow with a sly smile.

"Now, come on," said Sebastian. "I am not a vindictive man. All I wanted to do was thank the elf. I can't help it if he can't keep his balance in a simple boat. Here, let me give you a lift back into the row boat." Sebastian started to lift Elric but the little man didn't want his help.

"Don't touch me." Elric used his skinny little arms to pull himself upward. He stretched one leg over the side of the rowboat, almost back on board.

"Congratulations," called out Merrow's mother, waving from the boat.

"Yes, I agree," came the voice of her father. "Now, everyone back home through the portal. Right now." The Old Man of the Sea blew the Calling Conch, causing the portal to open up. It wasn't underwater, but atop the water this time. He dove through, and when he did, it caused a huge wave to tip the row boat over. Elric, Darium and Dee fell out and into the water.

Darium surfaced, laughing. Dee swam over to congratulate and hug Merrow. Elric's head popped up, and he looked like a drown rat. The elf was surely not happy.

"Damn it, I told you this was a bad idea," screamed Elric. "Someone get me out of this damned water. I can't swim."

"Take it easy, Elric," said Darium. "Hold on to the rowboat. I see The Thunderbolt coming to pick us up now."

Everyone had a good laugh and this time it was at the elf's expense.

"Merrow, I must leave now," said her mother. "Remember, just call to us in your mind if you want to visit and I'll send Nereus to open the portal."

"Thank you, Mother." Merrow hugged her, followed by hugs to Melite and Galene.

"We'll miss you, sister," said Melite.

Merrow brushed back a strand of her young sister's hair. "Just stay away from the Mystic Reef until I come to visit. I'll take you back then to look for more shells."

"I'll make certain she does," Galene promised.

"I can't wait that long." Melite pouted.

"Then I shall give you my shell necklace to wear until I return." Merrow took off her necklace and slipped it over Melite's head. Her sister's face lit up in a smile.

"I'll take good care of it, Merrow," said Melite.

"I know you will," Merrow answered. Merrow's hand closed over her shell charm that was fastened to her hair. Strangely, she could still feel that it was a part of her feelings and emotions. Sure enough, when she touched it, it glowed. "Mother, I thought when I married, my charm would hold no more power," she said in surprise.

"Remember, you're still a sea nymph," said Dee. "Your personal shell charm is there for your protection. Just don't lose it again."

"I won't take it, I promise," said Sebastian, using his fingers to make a cross over his heart. "Any passion coming from my wife from now on won't be because I am causing it to happen."

"Why, Husband," said Merrow, purposely trying to sound sexy. "I will hope my passion is indeed stirred up by you."

"You know what I mean," he whispered in her ear, kissing her atop her head, making Merrow giggle.

"You two make a wonderful couple," said Galene. "I hope the next wedding will be mine. I am sure you two will be very happy together."

"I know that we will," said Sebastian, giving the women hugs goodbye as well.

"Let us know as soon as the baby is born," said her mother as Galene and Melite helped her to swim to the portal.

"We will, Mother. I promise. Goodbye," called out Merrow, waving her hand over her head.

Merrow sadly watched as her family entered the portal one after another, and then the portal closed up behind them, leaving her alone once again.

"You're not sad to have to stay here on Mura, are you?" asked Sebastian.

Sebastian's ship approached the overturned rowboat. Rhys and Zann reached down to help the drenched sage up.

"You are all oafs, and haven't got a brain between you," whined Elric as they pulled him higher. "I'll expect three pazzleberry pies just for me now that this stupid excuse for a wedding is over. Zann, you're not pulling hard enough. Hurry. Or don't you have enough strength to even lift an elf from the sea?"

Merrow saw Zann exchange glances with Rhys before they let go of Elric. "Oops," said Zann as the sage once again fell back into the sea. A big splash and lots of swearing from Elric followed. The Blackseed brothers all laughed aloud.

"Sorry about that, Elric," Zann called out. "I guess you were right that I'm too weak to pull an elf from the sea. Mayhap you'd better swim back to shore."

"Dammit, you big oafs. This isn't funny. Now get me out of here," screamed Elric.

"Take it easy," Darium told him from the water. "Having a bath once a year isn't going to melt you, Elric."

That caused everyone on the ship to laugh again.

"To answer your question," Merrow said to Sebastian, "at first, I thought I might be sad staying here without my family. But the more I get to know the people of Mura and our new alliance friends, I realize that I am going to love living here after all." She burst out laughing when this time, Elric used his magic to knock Rhys and Zann into the water with him. The Blackseed brothers were all in the water now, and seemed to be enjoying it, splashing each other and making jests. That only infuriated Elric even more.

"I love you, Merrow," said Sebastian, holding her and kissing her while she used her tail to keep them afloat.

"I love you, too, Sebastian. And I can't wait for us to be parents." She kissed him back. "I must admit that when I first got sucked through the portal and got caught in your fishing net, I thought my life was over."

"Nay. Not at all," Sebastian told her. "Actually, it was nothing more than a new beginning. Destiny. Fate brought us together. A new life has begun between a sea nymph and a human, even though no one I know could have ever expected this union to exist."

"You're right," she said with a grin. "After all, our lives quickly came together in a way no one ever expected. I guess it was meant to be."

"That is the best kind," said Sebastian.

"Best kind? What does that mean?" she asked.

"Our lives, being so different from each other, melded together just fine after all," he assured her. "I say the best relationships are the ones that no one expects. We were so different, yet together, we realize we are really the same after all. Our lives are combined now, and that just makes us stronger. I have no doubt, sweetheart, that the best marriage takes place when two people like us allow our lives to become *Entangled*."

*From the Author*

I hope you enjoyed Merrow and Sebastian's story and will take a moment to leave a review for me.

Undines, or sea nymphs as they are also called are fascinating, magical creatures. I knew I had to bring one to Mura. In the Greek myths, Nereus is referred to by Homer as the Old Man of the Sea. He is seen to be a gentle sea god who is wise and can shapeshift. Stories about Poseidon, the sea god, claim that he is more aggressive and can even cause earthquakes.

My research shows Nereus as the son of Pontus (the sea) and Gaia (the earth). He lived in the Aegean Sea with his wife, Doris (I call her Dee) They had fifty sea nymph daughters and one son together.

It has been debated for eons whether Nereus is the same sea god as Poseidon or not. I am not sure if it has ever really been decided. But in my book, I chose to combine traits of both Nereus and Poseidon into one man. Or one god, shall I say?

Be sure to catch up with the entire **Portals of Destiny Series**. You don't want to miss all the escapades of those Blackseed brothers, as well as the ornery little elf, Elric. To see a full colorized map of the land of Mura,

please go to my website at **http://elizabethrosenovel
s.com.**

My **Elemental Magick Series** is related to this, and
is on the map as well. Characters from this series cross
over into my Portals of Destiny Series. Two more of my
series that might interest you are the **Tangled Tales** (my
heroine, Medea from **Bewitched** comes from this series) and also my **Greek Myth Fantasy Series**.

Watch for more books coming soon.

*Elizabeth Rose*

# About Elizabeth

Elizabeth Rose is an award-winning, bestselling author of over 100 books and counting. She writes medieval, historical, contemporary, paranormal, and western romance. Her books are available as EBooks, paperbacks, and some audiobooks as well.

Her favorite characters in her works include dark, dangerous and tortured heroes, and feisty, independent heroines who know how to wield a sword. She loves writing 14th century medieval novels, and is well-known for her many series.

Elizabeth loves the outdoors. In the summertime, you can find her in her secret garden with her laptop, swinging in her hammock working on her next book. Elizabeth is a born storyteller and passionate about sharing her works with her readers.

Please be sure to visit her website at **Elizabethrosenovels.com** to read excerpts from any of her novels and get sneak peeks at covers of upcoming books. You can follow her on **Twitter**, **Facebook**, **Goodreads** or **BookBub.** Join Elizabeth's **newsletter** so you don't miss out on new releases or upcoming events.

# Also by Elizabeth Rose

**Medieval Series:**
Legendary Bastards of the Crown Series
Seasons of Fortitude Series
Secrets of the Heart Series
Legacy of the Blade Series
Daughters of the Dagger Series
MadMan MacKeefe Series
Barons of the Cinque Ports Series
Holiday Knights Series
Highland Chronicles Series
Pirate Lords Series
Highland Outcasts

**Medieval/Paranormal Series:**
Elemental Magick Series
Greek Myth Fantasy Series
Tangled Tales Series
Portals of Destiny

**Contemporary Series:**
Tarnished Saints Series
Working Man Series

**Western Series:**
Cowboys of the Old West Series

**And More!**

Please visit http://elizabethrosenovels.com